MW01223992

What the critics are saying...

5 *Ribbons* "Arianna Hart has penned a galactic thrill ride that is guaranteed to bring out the futuristic romance lover in everyone." ~*Romance Junkies*

"REBEL'S LUST is a crazy, fast-paced space romp with plenty of action."~ *ecataromance*

REBEL'S LUST

By Arianna Hart

REBEL'S LUST
An Ellora's Cave Publication, December 2004

Ellora's Cave Publishing, Inc.
1337 Commerce Drive
Stow, Ohio 44224

ISBN # 1419951610
Other available formats: ISBN MS Reader (LIT), Adobe (PDF),
Rocketbook (RB), Mobipocket (PRC) & HTML

Rebel's Lust© 2004 Arianna Hart

ALL RIGHTS RESERVED. This book may not be reproduced in
whole or in part without permission.

This book is a work of fiction and any resemblance to persons,
living or dead, or places, events or locales is purely coincidental.
They are productions of the authors' imagination and used
fictitiously.

Edited by: *Briana St. James*
Cover art by: *Syneca*

Warning:

The following material contains graphic sexual content meant for mature readers. *Rebel's Lust* has been rated *E-rotic* by a minimum of three independent reviewers.

Ellora's Cave Publishing offers three levels of Romantica™ reading entertainment: S (S-ensuous), E (E-rotic), and X (X-treme).

S-*ensuous* love scenes are explicit and leave nothing to the imagination.

E-*rotic* love scenes are explicit, leave nothing to the imagination, and are high in volume per the overall word count. In addition, some E-rated titles might contain fantasy material that some readers find objectionable, such as bondage, submission, same sex encounters, forced seductions, etc. E-rated titles are the most graphic titles we carry; it is common, for instance, for an author to use words such as "fucking", "cock", "pussy", etc., within their work of literature.

X-*treme* titles differ from E-rated titles only in plot premise and storyline execution. Unlike E-rated titles, stories designated with the letter X tend to contain controversial subject matter not for the faint of heart.

Also available from Arianna Hart:

Federation Chronicles 1: Lucy's Lover
By Honor Bound *anthology*

REBEL'S LUST

By Arianna Hart

Prologue

"Delivery from the Empress Lisandra, you want to check it out Major?" the security officer at the receiving bay squawked over Lara's communicator.

Damn. Ten more minutes and her shift with Emperor "Touchy" Thomellt would be over and she could get some sleep. Lots of sleep. Twelve hours protecting the Emperor and dodging his fat-fingered attempts at groping were enough to make her want to hide in her bunk for a week.

"Yes, let me get Captain Drog to cover me with the Emperor and I'll be right down. What is it?"

"Looks like food."

"Okay, do a chemical scan of the crate and grab me a biological scanner too. I'll be down in a minute."

If she played her cards right she could debrief Drog, check out the packages, and still get into bed in under an hour. Signing off on the last of the orders, Lara closed the file on her hand held computer and crossed to the Emperor's door. Knocking politely, she waited for him to access the panel and open the door.

"Emperor Thomellt, Sire. A transport has arrived from Empress Lisandra. I'm going below to check it out. Captain Drog will be in charge for the remainder of the night."

"A package from my wife? What is it?"

"The security officer in receiving says it looks like food. I'm going to run a scan over it now to make sure it is safe."

"What could be safer than a package from my wife? Have the officer open it up and tell me what it is." The Emperor rubbed his piggy hands together in obvious gastric glee.

Lara gritted her teeth and called up the officer. "The Emperor would like you to open the delivery and tell him what it is. Do a quick scan first though."

"Roger that Major." There was a pause while the officer presumably did her bidding, and Touchy Thomellt eyed her body through her uniform. What had she ever done to deserve bodyguard duty?

"Looks like fresh protein, Major. Enough to feed the whole ship!"

"Fresh protein! Deliver it to the mess hall immediately! I'll send my own chef down to personally inspect it." The Emperor was almost drooling at the idea of fresh food after months of space rations.

"I think I should still check it out—"

"Nonsense! This is a gift from my loving wife. I won't stand for such an insult. Send me my chef, I want to discuss the menu with him personally."

"Yes, Sire." *You bloated excuse for a human being. I hope the meat constipates you for a week.*

Lara executed a sharp pivot and left the Emperor to wax poetic about eating dead animals. As soon as she got in the hall outside the Emperor's quarters, she flipped up her communicator again.

"Drog?" Lara waited for a response. He should be on his way to the guardroom now since his shift started in a few minutes. Why the hell wasn't he answering?

"Drog, come in? Where are you?"

"Uh, I'm, uh, coming now, Major."

Lara could hear grunts and moans as Drog forgot to shut his end down. She could clearly hear a woman's voice screaming, "Fuck me, fuck me now!" Mercifully, the connection was cut before Lara had to hear whether or not the woman got her wish.

Five minutes later, Drog stumbled out of the maintenance closet down the hall, a satisfied smile on his face.

"So glad you could make it for your shift, Captain."

Drog looked startled at her presence in the hallway, but quickly recovered. Lieutenant Malone walked out of the closet behind him, fixing her hair as she did up the front of her medical uniform.

"Major, I was on my way."

"Spare me, Drog. Kindly confine your extracurricular activities to your own time, not mine. The Emperor is getting a shipment of protein. I'm going to check it out. You are in charge until oh eight hundred tomorrow."

"Yes, Ma'am."

Lara shot the Chief Medical Officer a look until she smiled and walked away, then transferred the door codes to Drog's communicator. After a parting shot about keeping his mind on the job she left to do the scan on the shipment against orders.

It went against her nature to ignore a direct order, but her job was to keep the Emperor safe. Even if that meant she had to keep him safe from himself. Stumbling with weariness, Lara walked into the receiving bay only to see the remains of a shipping crate strewn about the floor.

"What the hell is going on here?" she shouted to the first uniformed grunt she could find.

"When word got out that we had fresh protein, the mess crew came down and practically tore the place apart trying to get the choicest cuts. Then the Emperor's chef and his snooty assistant came in and took their share too."

"Did you scan it at least?"

"That I did, Ma'am. No unusual chemical readings at all."

"Did you check for biological abnormalities?"

"There was a slight elevation in the bio scan, but nothing that a few minutes on the grill won't take care of."

Lara wasn't so sure about that, but the scanner would have indicated if the biological readings were too high and even the hungriest of cooks wouldn't take protein that had gone bad.

"For your sake I hope you're right." She gave him the best threatening glance she could muster while her head was spinning with exhaustion, then turned and headed for bed.

Chapter One

The beeping of her monitor woke Lara out of a dead sleep. Rubbing gritty eyes, she tried to read the time on the wall clock. Damn, she'd only been asleep two hours.

"What? This had better be good," she growled into the communicator on her wrist monitor.

Lara waited for a response. Nothing, just the sound of an open communicator. She was about to turn the thing off and pitch it across the room when the sound of violent retching came on the line. Her own stomach rolled in sympathy. Finally she heard a moan and a weak gasping whisper.

"Major, I'm sick. Can't protect Emperor, need backup," Drog groaned.

"Well, then call someone! Follow the chain of command. You know what it is. Who's next on rotation?" For stars' sake why did he have to call her? Drog was a veteran, he knew the drill.

"Can't, everyone sick. Even the Emperor and his doctor..." There was a pause and more retching.

"Great, just great. I love dealing with puking officers on two hours of sleep."

Lara threw the covers off, swung her feet to the floor and stood up with a stretch. She grabbed her suit off the foot of her bunk and slipped it on without her usual undergarments. With any luck at all she'd find someone on the rotation that wasn't sick and she'd be able to go back to sleep. If she were really lucky no one would notice the fact that her breasts were jutting out in front of her like the prow of a ship because she didn't have a bra on.

She was about to turn off her monitor since the sound of Drog tossing his cookies wasn't doing wonders for her own stomach when the ship shuddered.

Alarm bells and sirens wailed, lights flashed, and the automatic warning system announced its message of danger in its ever so annoyingly calm voice.

"Warning, the ship has been breached. Hull damage in sector twenty-nine. Warning, the ship has been breached. Hull damage in sector twenty-nine."

Lara started to run. She was in sector ten, and Drog was with the Emperor in sector nineteen. The map of the ship she had memorized when she first got this assignment ran through her head. She'd need to go through the mess hall and down two flights of stairs to get to the Emperor before whoever attacked the ship did.

Cutting through the mess hall and sprinting down the stairs, she briefly registered the smell of human waste and vomit permeating the entire ship. What the hell was going on? Was everyone sick? Not a crewmember moved except to lean weakly over and hurl some more. The floor was slippery with stars only knew what, making her sprint that much more difficult.

As she took the stairs to sector nineteen she heard the blast of laser fire. She rounded the corner and saw Drog was on the ground in front of the Emperor's door, using one of the ridiculous ornamental dogs that flanked the entryway as a shield. Even as Lara dove to help him, it was too late. Drog fired one last weak shot from his laser before he misjudged his cover and took a hit to the shoulder that spun him around.

He didn't get up.

Lara remained crouched near the second dog. So far she didn't think they saw her, whoever they were. If she played her cards right she might be able to surprise them before they got their hands on the Emperor. The door to his room was coded and sealed, it wouldn't survive a laser cannon, but it should slow them down for a while.

Come on, come on show yourselves! Lara waited breathlessly for them to make their next move. They had to be going for the Emperor, he was the only thing of value on this stupid ship. She'd think about who would want to risk the wrath of the United Galaxies later, right now she had to protect the Emperor at all costs.

Another laser blast took the head off the dog where Drog had been hiding. They were making sure he was down for the count. Stars, she hoped not. Drog was smart enough to stay down and play dead. Lara took another look at his inert body, praying that he was only acting. Her eyes watered as she stared at him, afraid to blink and miss a breath. Finally, when she thought her own heart would burst from lack of oxygen, she saw the shallow rise and fall of Drog's chest.

He was alive! It was up to her to make sure he stayed that way.

She held tight to her location, waiting for the attackers to make the next move. Finding her center, Lara tensed and released her muscles in preparation for sudden movement. This was no time for her muscles to get stiff.

Two black-clad enemy soldiers scurried to the doorway of the guardroom to search for opposition.

Obviously they didn't find any because the scouts signaled back and carried on. Lara waited for them to start firing at the Emperor's door; she could probably take out a few before they realized the door was firing back.

Only they didn't fire at the door.

Before Lara could react they had the door coded and opened and were signaling back again. Lara sprang from her hiding space and took out the assailant closest to the door with a spear-hand poke to the kidney and a chop to the neck. The second one got a kick in the side of the head before he could even figure out what was happening.

Where the hell was the Emperor? Lara raced through the room, laser at the ready, only to find the fat slob whimpering in his lake of a bed, covered in his own vomit.

"Come on, Sire. You have to come with me. Your life is in danger." Lara tried to help him out of the bed, but it was like dragging dead weight through mud.

"I'm already dying. Can't you see? I'm dying and no one can help me, we're all doomed." He flopped back onto the bed, moaning piteously into his fur-covered bedspread.

"Sire, please. I know you aren't feeling well, but we must get you to an escape pod before it is too late." Lara pulled his arm with all her might. The Emperor was not a tall man, but he weighed nearly as much as someone twice his height. She wasn't small by any stretch of the imagination, but there was no way she could lift him out of the bed and carry him to the escape pod. "Sire, I need your help to save you. You must get out of this bed so you can escape to safety."

The Emperor's response was drowned out by the blast of a laser fired over her head. Lara threw her body in front of the Emperor and returned fire. She had no shield to protect her from their blasts; she was acting as a living shield.

Lara fired her laser as fast as it could recharge. Men were coming in the room faster than she could take them out. These were trained professionals, she thought as she tried to block the Emperor's body with her own. He wasn't making her job any easier, rolling around and squealing like a pig every time she shot the laser. She felt the bed move under her as he beached himself on the other side, but didn't have time to react to the motion before his movements threw her off the bed.

Fifteen years of martial arts training, five years in special arms training, and she ended up landing in a heap on the floor. Some bodyguard she was. She scrambled up to guard the Emperor, but two men got there before her and dragged him out the door. Two more attackers came at her, their hands held up at a guard and their weight balanced on the balls of their feet. These guys were definitely well-trained.

Lara needed to take these guys out and fast. She didn't want to get into a prolonged battle with them when her Emperor was being dragged who knew where. The goon on the left pulled his laser out of his belt and aimed for her head. Lara dropped down and swept his leg out from under him. The laser went flying as he fell, clattering against the floor.

The second one rushed her, trying to grab her before she got up, but she rolled to the side and got to her feet quickly. The men began circling her, trying to get her in the middle of them. Perfect.

She waited until they got close enough for her to make contact, then crouched down low, only to spring up and get both of them with a scissor kick. She'd always wondered if that would really work.

Not wasting any time patting herself on the back, Lara charged out into the hallway. Four more men where taking rear guard and shot their lasers at her. She dove out of the way and rolled to the closet where Drog had been going at it earlier. Lara crawled into the tiny shelter and climbed up the shelves. She was almost positive there was an entry to the ventilation ducts in here for the maintenance workers to use.

Where the hell was the latch? Her fingers flew over the ceiling, groping around for a seam like a blind woman. Damn! Something cut her hand. The latch! Fumbling with the tiny but painful piece of metal, Lara finally managed to get it open. Using her arms to pull herself up, she clawed her way into the duct and took a minute to plan her route.

They had to have ships; if that were the case they'd either be heading to the hanger or to the breach. Too bad they were at opposite ends of the ship. She had to make a choice, and make it quick.

The hanger. Even if she was wrong, she'd be able to grab a speeder and follow them until she could summon help. Decision made, Lara wasted no more time, but slithered along the network of ducts as fast as she could go on her elbows and knees. Good thing the suit was as slippery as it was tight or she'd never get anywhere.

Trying to judge her distance while crawling through inches of dust in the ventilation ducts was harder than she had expected when she'd hatched this plan. Running through the corridors from one end of the ship to the other was one thing, crawling on elbows and knees with her boobs getting in the way and sneezing her head off was a totally different situation.

Lara listened for movement below her. If she had judged correctly, she'd be just above the main bay in the hanger. If she hadn't judged correctly, she was in for a long fall.

Opening the nearest hatch in the ventilation duct, she peered down to see if she could find the catwalk that ran over the bay. Damn, she was too far over. The catwalk was probably four feet away. There must be another ventilation shaft that was closer, but she didn't have time to back track to find it. She looked around to see if there were any signs of the kidnappers, but the bay was eerily silent. She still needed to get down to the ground, and the only way was the catwalk, which was tantalizingly out of reach.

It was only a few feet away, but she had no way to lean over from inside the ventilation duct. Wiping her dusty hands off on her suit, Lara griped the edge of the opening and swung her body as far as she could towards the catwalk. Her foot slammed into the metal frame with an earsplitting clang. Great! Why didn't she just shout out "Here I am, shoot me please!" Getting a better grip, she swung again, this time catching the rail with her legs.

Now what?

Her arms were pulling painfully over her head, and her knees were gripping the railing like there was no tomorrow, while the rest of her almost six foot frame was hanging in the middle. She really needed to think these things through a little better.

Taking a deep breath and praying to the powers that be, Lara let go of her death grip on the ventilation entry hatch. Her legs screamed in pain as the full weight of her body swung down. The railing gave a heart-wrenching lurch, but held firm. Now came the truly painful part. Inch by excruciating inch, Lara used her stomach muscles to pull herself up far enough to grab the railing with her hands. She might actually have to thank her old drill sergeant for making her do a million sit-ups during basic.

Once her hands had found purchase on the railing, it was easy enough to slip over to the safe side of the catwalk. If one could call a two-foot wide metal walkway suspended over a hundred feet of open space safe. Getting her bearings, she looked around the cavernous hanger for any signs of the attackers' passing.

Either they hadn't gotten there yet, which wasn't very likely considering how much time it took her to get there, or they went out the breach. Damn! She'd have to follow them and call for backup.

Lara jogged across the metal platform, her boots clanging like a gong with every step. When she got to the ladder, she slid her sleeves over her hands, gripped the rails, and slid down. The fabric kept her hands from getting chewed up by the friction and it was so slippery, she got down in seconds.

Grabbing a ration pack, flight suit, and breathing apparatus, Lara hopped into the fastest speeder she could find. She wouldn't be fighting the attackers as much as following them, and stealth and speed would be more valuable than firepower. Flipping on the warm-up switches she waited anxiously for the aircraft to go through its torturous start-up procedures. Minutes felt like decades while she waited for the speeder to power up. The thing could practically fly itself, which was good, because a pilot she was not. She could handle a small bird like this, but she wouldn't be winning any races in it.

Pressing the button to open the hanger doors, Lara turned the scanners on full tilt. She needed to find the ion trail that the attackers would have left. If she could find that she'd be able to follow them until they went into hyperdrive. She hoped.

"This is Major Lara McDaniel from the Emperor's cruiser *The Federation* calling an all-points bulletin. Emperor Thomellt has been abducted. All hands on *The Federation* are either dead or incapacitated. I am in pursuit going…" Where was she going anyway? The scanners showed ion trails going towards the Beta Quadrant. Great. She was going into hell's mouth. "I am in pursuit going towards the Beta Quadrant, repeat, following ion trails of the abductors towards the Beta Quadrant. Will advise when I have more information. Over." Lara set the message on repeat, and pushed it out of her mind. Someone was bound to hear it sooner or later.

The kidnappers weren't even trying to hide their trail, which meant either they didn't think she'd follow them or it was a trick. With the way her luck was running today, it probably would be a trap. Well, she had no choice but to follow them.

Two hours later, Lara found a dump of space debris floating in the middle of the ion trail. That didn't make any sense, unless they dumped their garbage to save fuel. Zipping around the mass of flotsam she never saw the blast that hit her tail. Damn it, she knew it was a trap. A second blast rocked her ship and her world went black.

Chapter Two

"Well Max, what have we got here? Looks like someone did a purge before hitting hyperdrive. We've got ourselves a gold mine of salvage ripe for the picking!"

Max didn't answer. He seldom did more than swish his tail at Riley's ramblings anyway, and the idea of a boatload of metal didn't seem to excite him in the least.

"You know, you could show a little enthusiasm, buddy. This is our livelihood, and if I don't make money, you don't get fed." Riley looked at the twenty-pound cat and snorted. "Not that you need to eat anymore anyway. If you moved any less I could use you for ballast."

Riley continued his monologue while setting the tractor beam to haul in the greatest amount of debris for the least amount of drag. He carefully locked down the cargo bay door that stood between the bay and the rest of the ship before pulling in the haul. There was always the chance of finding something explosive in a huge haul like this, but then what was life without a few risks?

When the catch of the day was landed, Riley gave out a whoop of triumph. This load ought to sell for enough to keep him sitting pretty for a few months. He'd blow it all on cards, booze, and women, but hey what was the use of having money if he couldn't enjoy it? He initiated the scan and waited to see what treasures were to be found amidst the rubble.

"Life form detected, repeat, life form detected," the sex kitten voice of his computer announced, jolting him out of his avarice.

"What do you mean life form? Nothing could survive out there." Damn, if this was a shipwreck then he'd have to split the haul with the survivor. There were pirates out there who would kill any survivors to avoid splitting the booty, but he wasn't one of them. Too damn bad.

"Bonny, what kind of life form, and is there anything in there radioactive or explosive?" Riley's ship was actually named *The Donegal*, but had transformed into the Bonny Girl over time. He'd gotten her and Max from an ailing space smuggler years ago. Over the years she'd become more than a ship to him. She and Max were his only family, and that was just fine by him.

"Scanning…"

Riley tapped his foot at the delay. He had a prime haul here, and even if he had to split it, he'd still make a bundle. But it was his haul and he didn't like sharing.

"Human life form. Negative radioactive readings. Negative chemical readings indicating explosive probabilities."

"Good enough for me." Riley pressurized the cargo area and unlocked the door when the green light indicated it was safe to do so. He pulled his laser out of his boot and held it down low next to him. Just because he wouldn't kill on sight, didn't mean the person in there wouldn't either.

Max's tail bristled out to twice its normal size at the first sniff of the haul. He hissed and arched his back, his ears flattened in fury.

"What is it, fella? What's wrong? You don't move this much unless you see a dog, or smell…shit." He pushed his way into the clumps of metal. Max was a Gamma Cat, a breed of cat specifically bred for space travel. And for sensing the gamma particle trails left by Traminian laser blasts. Whoever was in there was in deep doo-doo if they had been shot at by Traminian ships.

Chances are they were already dead. He could just jettison this load and forget he ever saw it. He hadn't logged his claim yet, so there was no reason he *had* to go any further. The last thing he wanted was to get involved with anything having to do with Traminians or their damn blasters.

Then why was he digging through space rubble like a madman?

Grabbing a hook from the wall, Riley pulled apart the haul looking for something that would have been worth shooting at. If Bonny hadn't said there was a life form in here, he would think that maybe some Traminian boys were just having a little fun shooting at space junk.

But she did say there was a life form here.

Damn.

Riley continued to dig his way deeper and deeper. He was about ready to give up when the hook caught on the mangled tail of a speedster. And this was no ordinary speedster if he remembered correctly. More junk was pushed off as he got a closer look. This bird had the Emperor of Emeraldia's crest on it.

This was getting worse and worse. Exposing the cockpit of the craft, he pressed the emergency release lever and got his first look at what the Traminians had been shooting at.

Damn, his grandmother always told him bad news came in threes. Looked like she was right again. Bad enough that there was a live body in the wreckage, but to be a woman, and one who was being shot at by Traminians, that just couldn't be good. Some days it just didn't pay to be a good guy.

The woman in the cockpit started to stir. Riley pulled off her helmet to help her breathe. There was a lump on her head the size of his fist. Whoever she was, she needed help. But damn it, why did he have to be the one to give it? Why couldn't he have just gone on by the tempting pile of space junk in his path? He was born under an unlucky star, he just knew it. A woman would mean nothing but trouble.

And damn, but he had enough trouble all on his own, he didn't need to borrow any more. He'd help out this spacer-babe because he had no choice, but then he'd ditch her at the first space station he came across.

"Come on, Sweet Cheeks, let's get you fixed up," Riley said as he heaved her out of the speedster. She certainly wasn't petite. The only way he could carry her was to throw her over his shoulder. That wouldn't do much for her head injury, but he didn't have much of a choice.

Flipping her over his shoulder like a load of ballast, Riley stumbled into the cabin. He dropped her on the bunk as gently as he could under the circumstances.

"Bonny, I need freeze-packs and some clean-wipes, and do we have extra thermo-blankets? I don't remember."

"Sending them to you now." The soothing voice did very little to calm his nerves.

He knew that with head wounds the first thing was to stabilize the neck. Too late for that now. The next thing would be to put some freeze-packs on the lump. That he could do. While he waited for the freeze-packs he took a better look at his unwanted passenger. She had a thick braid of brown hair that was so long it fell to the floor. The skintight spacesuit showed off breasts that the strippers on Epsilon would envy. She was tall, probably close to his six feet two inches. She had muscles beneath those curves though; this wasn't someone's arm piece, that was for sure.

Riley leaned over to get the supplies Bonny sent from the kitchen to the tube by his bed and caught a glimpse of the insignia on his patient's sleeve. He let out a low whistle between his teeth. What he had here was an honest to goodness Major of the Imperial Army. Huh, what was a major doing in a speedster, amidst a bunch of space junk in the Beta Quadrant? He hadn't seen a military transport nearby, and what would the Emperor of Emeraldia be doing in this armpit of space? He was going to have to wait until his guest woke up to find out.

Meanwhile, he'd uncover some more of this mystery, by uncovering her. Riley sat down on the bed and looked for a zipper or a catch to open the spacesuit. The thing was all one piece as far as he could tell. There wasn't a seam on it, and when he experimented with his knife, he couldn't so much as tear a thread off it. Was it painted on?

That might be a job worth having, he thought as his eyes trailed over every curve of her body. Laying a coat of paint over that body would be tops on his dream job list. His dick picked this time to remind him it had been months since he'd visited the houses on Epsilon. That's just what he needed, a spacer-babe in skintight clothes, that he couldn't get rid of, who happened to be a major in the Imperial Army.

Just when he was considering his intelligence in not dumping the whole load immediately, she woke up. Dark brown eyes looked at him in confusion, pain, and not a little bit of anger.

"Where am I? Who are you? And what the hell is going on?"

And he thought things couldn't get much worse before. Now he had bossy to add to the list.

"You are on my ship, *the Bonny*—uh, *The Donegal*. I'm the captain and crew and the guy who saved your ass from getting blown out of the sky by Traminian flyboys. Name's Riley."

"Major Lara McDaniel, Commander of the Emperor's personal guards. Or at least I was."

"How'd a bodyguard end up in a speedster in Beta Quad?"

"Before I tell you anything, how do you know it was Traminians?" She looked at him like he was some sort of bug and she couldn't decide if he was dangerous or just disgusting.

Riley covertly looked at himself in the reflection of the metal plate over the bunk. Okay, so his hair was getting a little long, and he hadn't shaved in a few days. Maybe more than a few. His shirt was missing some buttons, and there was a tear in the knee of his pants. He wasn't exactly up to inspection, but he had just saved her ass. She could at least show some appreciation.

He pushed himself off the bed and sat down in the chair next to it. Being on the same bed with all those curves made thinking straight more than a little difficult. "Trust me, I've been around. I know blasts from

Traminian particle cannons, and that is what you got hit with."

"But they're our allies! Why would they kidnap the Emperor?" she asked softly, more to herself than him.

"Wait a minute. You're saying whoever did this to your ship kidnapped the Emperor?"

"I didn't say that!" Her brown eyes lasered back into his.

"You sure as hell did."

"I don't know who shot at me, but it doesn't make any sense for the Traminians to fire on an Imperial ship."

"Nope, but trust me, I know what I'm talking about."

"You keep telling me to trust you, why should I? You dress like a slob, the condition of your ship leaves something to be desired, and you look like you haven't seen another human in eons. No, trusting you is not something I plan on doing any time soon."

She tried to stand up, but immediately sat back down. Good, he hoped her head was killing her. So what if he didn't keep his appearance up to military standards? He'd had enough of that when he was in the army. Maybe the ship could use a cleaning, but that didn't mean he didn't know what he was talking about.

"Would you sit back down and listen a second, Sweet Cheeks? You see that beast over there masquerading as a cat?" he said, indicating Max who was washing his genitals in the middle of the room. "That there is a Gamma Cat. Smugglers and pirates have been breeding them for years because they can sense the gamma particles that come off Traminian weapons. The minute I opened the bay door his hair stood up like he'd been electrocuted.

That's how I know you've been shot at by Traminians." He sat back and crossed his arms over his chest.

"Figures you're a smuggler and a pirate."

"It doesn't matter what I am, I'm all you've got right now."

"What's that supposed to mean?"

"It means that I'm the only thing standing between you and a painful death out there in open space. It also means you had better be nice to me until I can drop you at the nearest space station."

"Not a chance, Flyboy. The Emperor has been abducted and you are going to help me get him back." It was her turn to sit back smugly and cross her arms over her chest.

"Not *fecking* likely, babe. You should be glad you are getting a free ride to Epsilon Station and not booted into space." There was no way in hell he was going to go tearing off on some wild goose chase with the entire Traminian army on his tail.

"Oh I think it is quite likely. You see, I'm a member of the Imperial Army, on a mission of life or death that affects the security of the United Galaxies. Galaxy bylaw 197-42 states that any ship flying in Federation Space that encounters a member of the Imperial Army or one of its allies in life or death need shall be commandeered, at the owners expense, until such a time as it is no longer needed."

"*Toradal-shit!*"

"Failure to obey said law will result in a permanent suspension of one's license and immediate confiscation of one's ship."

She looked even more smug, if that was possible. There wasn't a chance in hell he was risking his life and livelihood to go after some damn Emperor. There had to be some loophole to this.

"Bonny! Did Major McDaniel give me the correct information?" Riley waited for Bonny to answer him. He'd find out the truth now.

"Not completely," the voice purred into the room.

"Hah! See, I knew there was a way out of this. Go ahead, Bonny, tell me what she left out." Let's see if she was so smug now. Bet she didn't think he had backup for her little gamma bomb.

"The Major forgot to add that there is an additional fine of one thousand credits levied on any spacecraft that does not comply with bylaw number 197-42."

Riley stood there, stunned worse than if he'd been hit with a laser.

"So what do you have to eat, 'partner'?" she drawled.

Chapter Three

Lara looked at the scruffy space pirate and tried to hide her smirk. He kept running his hand through his sandy colored hair, and his green eyes were wide in astonishment and shock. He looked like he'd been run over by a herd of *toradals*. Served him right, arrogant Flyboy. She had a job to do and this sorry excuse for a human being wasn't going to blow it. It had taken years of working harder, longer, and doing all the shit jobs to earn the rank of Major, and she wasn't going to get bucked back down to Private because he didn't feel cooperative.

"Can't we work some sort of deal here?" he asked a little less belligerently.

"Sure, you can take me back to Emeraldia and I can gather enough troops to find and rescue the Emperor."

"I can't fly you all the way back to Emeraldia! That's on the other side of the *fecking* galaxy!" He threw up his hands in obvious frustration.

"Then I guess it looks like we are going to follow the ion trail, if there still is one."

"Don't you get it? You can't just go flying blindly off into space following ion trails. I'm sure there more than one ship, and I'm sure they are all laying false trails for you to follow in case you survived the first attack. A condition that is still questionable I might add!"

"Well, I can't just lay here and do nothing. I need to find my Emperor!"

"Is he such a great guy that you're willing to risk your life for him?"

"He's a sexist prick but it's my job!"

"Then do your job and think this through. How did they get him off the ship? Blast, how did they get on the ship in the first place? An Emperor's cruiser is no party ship, there is a major arsenal on board that thing. Where were all the scouts?"

"Puking their guts out. As far as I could tell, everyone on board the ship was either sick or poisoned."

"How could that happen? Doesn't the Emperor carry his own rations?"

Lara had an uneasy stirring in her gut. For a whole ship to get poisoned at once it would mean an inside job. But who? Who on board her ship would do something like that? She was trying to concentrate, but her head was killing her, and Riley's presence was doing weird things to her body. As he stood up, she got an up close and personal look at the package between his legs. And if that wasn't impressive enough, when he bent over to pick the monster cat up off the floor his black pants clung to his butt like her *fecking* spacesuit. She'd like to get a look at him in one of the skintight uniforms the staff of *The Federation* had to wear. Her eyes strayed to the region below his waist. Yeah, she'd definitely like to see him in one of those suits.

What the stars was she thinking? She must have gotten hit harder than she thought. She was ogling some lowlife while her Emperor was being taken halfway across the cosmos. What had he asked her? Oh yeah, the poison.

"I don't know what poison they could have used to make everyone but me sick. I breathe the same air, drink the same water, eat the same—that's it!"

"What's it?"

"We got a special delivery from the Empress. She sent a shipload of meat, the real stuff. The whole sparking ship was thrilled about fresh protein. Maybe the meat was poisoned?"

"Did you run any scans?"

"Chemical and biological. They came up negative, but I didn't do them personally." Damn it this was her fault. She should have double-checked the readings.

"Why didn't you eat any? Fresh protein is a luxury not many spacer grunts get very often."

How did he know so much about the military? Maybe there was more here than met the eye.

"I had just gotten off my shift; I grabbed a protein bar and hit the sack. I was too tired to fight my way through the crowd that was headed to the mess hall. Everyone was ecstatic about eating dead animals. I just wanted to sleep."

"So you were probably the only one who didn't eat the meat."

"I guess so." Stars, Lara prayed she wasn't the only one to survive. There were thousands of crewmembers on board *The Federation*, and her heart went cold thinking about their fate. The ship could repair itself from the breach, but it couldn't fly itself indefinitely. Her troops were on board that ship! What if they flew into hostile fire? Did she save her Emperor or her men?

"No." Riley shot an arrogant frown at her.

"What do you mean no? I haven't even said anything yet."

"You didn't have to. I know what you are thinking. Do you go back and try to save the ship? The answer is no."

"That's my crew on that ship and I'm not going to leave them flying around in space for any sparking pirate to come along and kill them. Don't you get it? They're out there floating around helpless, for stars' sake!"

"Yup, and there isn't a damn thing you can do about it now. Can you fly the ship alone? Can you treat thousands of sick crewmembers? Can you defend the ship from further attacks? No, you can't, so concentrate on doing what you can and let's make a plan."

"*Toradal-shit*! What the hell do you know about loyalty to a crew? I have a responsibility to make sure they're safe."

"You don't know dick about me, Sweet Cheeks."

"Nor do I want to. All I want is to save my Emperor, my crew, and my job."

"And you can't do all three at once. You have to focus on what you can reasonably accomplish, not on what your heart is telling you to do."

"I'm a professional; I don't let my emotions rule my decisions." How dare he accuse her of letting her emotions sway her?

"Then face the facts. You can't save both your crew and your Emperor."

How could she choose between one life and thousands? Her job was to protect her Emperor, but she was responsible for the soldiers that served under her.

"Look, even if you go back for your ship, chances are you wouldn't be able to save them anyway."

Was he right? She couldn't fly a space cruiser by herself; she could barely fly a speedster. And how would she take care of a thousand vomiting crewmembers? It galled her to admit it, but he was probably right. She needed to focus her energies where they would do the most good. And that was finding her Emperor.

"Fine. Let's make a plan. I say we follow the nearest ion trail and have that fat cat over there tell us when we are close to gamma cannons so we don't get blasted out of space. Maybe if we're lucky we can capture one of the bastards and find out where they are taking the Emperor."

"That's your plan? Just go bumping around space blindly until we run into them and pray we don't get killed?"

When he put it like that it sounded pretty stupid, but she wasn't thinking clearly at the moment. She'd had all of two hours of sleep before Drog woke her up; she'd been in hand-to-hand combat, shot at, had to slither through ventilation ducts, had hung over a hundred feet of open space, and then got knocked unconscious. He could cut her a little slack. "Well do you have a better plan?"

"As a matter of fact I do." He stretched, showing an impressive amount of firm abs, and crossed the room to stand by the door.

She had to get her mind off his body. *Focus on the job, McDaniel.* "Then let's hear it, Flyboy."

"We're going to go to Epsilon Station and get us some information." He crossed his arms over his chest and leaned back against the door. Lara noticed the muscles bulge in his arms as he waited for her response.

"Why are you suddenly so helpful? I thought it wasn't '*fecking* likely' that you would help me in the first place."

"I've been thinking—"

"Funny, I didn't smell smoke."

"I've been thinking that if we did manage to rescue the Emperor, there might be a nice little reward in it for me. Seems to me, saving someone as high and mighty as the Emperor ought to bag me enough credits to keep me in booze and babes for a few years. At least until I get bored."

"I should have known you'd be in it for yourself. Fine, whatever gets you to help me end this association as soon as possible. We'll head to Epsilon Station and get some information. But I'm warning you, if you think you are going to ditch me there I'll track you down to the ends of the galaxy and wear your balls as earrings."

"I have another place you can wear my balls, but we'll discuss that another time. You had better get some shuteye. We won't hit Epsilon for two days." He left the room without another word.

Lara watched him go with a sneer on her face until the door shut, then she collapsed back into the bunk with a groan. How did she end up in this mess?

She had transferred the codes to Captain Drog, did the most cursory of checks on the meat, and stumbled off to her bunk. Was it only a few hours ago? Stars, her biggest worry was whether or not she'd chew out Drog for playing slap and tickle in the supply closet, and avoiding Thomellt's greasy hands. Now she didn't know if her whole crew was dead or alive, what had happened to her Emperor, or who was behind the whole conspiracy.

How could things have gone so wrong so fast? Damn it! It was her job to make sure something like this didn't happen. If all lives on board *The Federation* were lost, it would be on her soul. Anxiety raced through her system as she thought about Drog lying wounded with no help in sight, but what could she have done differently? It was her job to guard the Emperor, Drog's too. He wouldn't have wanted her to rescue him and leave the Emperor defenseless.

Not that her defense did much good anyway. She'd given up her crew for her Emperor and didn't have either one. She was left with a reluctant Flyboy for a partner on a crumbling ship in the middle of nowhere. Her Commanding Officer would tear her up one side and down the other if he didn't kill her outright for this fiasco.

She couldn't think like this! Self-defeating thoughts wouldn't get her Emperor back. Right now she was in pain and sick to her stomach. After she got some sleep and healed a bit, she'd come up with a plan for rescuing her Emperor *and* the crew of *The Federation*. She'd do her job or die trying.

Climbing unsteadily out of the bed, she pressed the release on the inside collar of her suit, and breathed a sigh of relief as it dropped to the floor. The skintight material spilled from her body like a midnight blue puddle. It really was a marvel of modern science, but couldn't they have made the thing a little less revealing?

The suit could withstand, heat, cold, chemicals, and sharp objects. It never wrinkled, didn't get dirty or absorb sweat, and could even be used for a spacesuit in case of emergency. But the sparking thing left absolutely nothing to the imagination. Back on *The Federation*, every member of the crew wore one so it didn't matter so much. She had still taken to binding her breasts down so that men would talk to her and not her chest, but then again they had their own issues.

Wearing the suit in front of Riley made her feel naked. And aroused. She must have really taken a hit to the head. She didn't have much experience in the relationship department, but even she could tell that Riley had "No Trespassing" signs up all over him. That suited her just fine. She'd do her job, get the Emperor back, and hopefully save her ass while she was at it.

Climbing back into the bed, she thought about how he looked as he moved around the room. His panther-like grace, his tight ass, and impressive body. She could smell his musky scent on the pillows and blanket. She pulled the blanket up a little higher and let the fragrance permeate her senses.

What the hell was she doing? Hadn't she just figured out Riley was a waste of her time? And here she was sniffing his blankets like a *limfa* in heat. Man, this situation was going from bad to worse. She couldn't afford to let a loose cannon like him interfere with her job.

Breathing deeply of Riley's scent, her hands drifted over her body, teasing and tweaking her nipples before drifting down to the nest of curls between her legs. In the privacy of her dreams she could allow herself to think about him in ways she'd never admit to in the light of day. Picturing his sleek, muscular body over hers, Lara parted the slick folds of her cleft and felt for her clit.

As she rubbed the sensitive nubbin, she imagined Riley's hands on her breasts, squeezing and pinching her nipples before he sucked them into his mouth. Using her free hand, Lara teased her nipples some more, sending the blood rushing straight to her already sensitized core. Her pussy lips were dripping with juices as the pressure built between her legs.

In her mind, Riley worked his way down her body until his mouth was over her clit. Shoving a finger inside her tight sheath, she drove it in and out while fantasizing about Riley licking and sucking her aching clit. With his scent surrounding her and his body branded on her memory, Lara's body exploded. Her hips bucked against her hand as her release ended all too soon.

Rolling over and snuggling into Riley's pillow, she couldn't help but wish it was his hot body she was curled up against instead.

Chapter Four

Who would have thought the United Galaxies had become so *fecking* interfering? Used to be as long as a guy minded his own business, paid his taxes, and kept his nose clean no one bothered him. Now, just because he was in the wrong place at the wrong time he was stuck trying to rescue some *fecking* Emperor and take care of a *fecking* woman. He wanted to take her all right, but not the way she had in mind.

Riley took another pull on his syntho-beer. It didn't help. Launching himself out of the pilot's chair he paced the miniscule cockpit. There just had to be a way out of this. Somehow he was going to get his life back on course, and that didn't include a bossy, mouthy spacer-babe as a passenger.

The video telecaster had been set on low while he paced, he really didn't want Miss High and Mighty to wake up earlier than she had to. She had been asleep for twenty-four hours straight. He was going to have to wake her up soon just so he could get a little sleep himself. The chair conformed to his body, but it just wasn't the same as stretching flat out in his own bunk. The very bunk a naked Major Lara High and Mighty McDaniel was sleeping in around the clock. He was about to turn the video monitor off completely when the Emperor's picture appeared on the screen.

"Bonny, turn up the volume three decibels," Riley said, sitting in his seat for a closer look.

"Word from the palace is not good. The Empress Lisandra has had no word of the Emperor's whereabouts, and kidnappers have not issued any ransom demands. Sources from inside the palace are stating the lives of the entire crew aboard *The Federation* have been lost. Imperial police are looking for the whereabouts of any space-farer who was in the Beta Quadrant or its vicinity in the last twenty-four hours."

The screen flashed a picture of the Emperor getting on the cruiser, and Riley could have sworn he saw a glimpse of a dark brown braid in the background. He wondered how long her hair was when it isn't wound up tight as a whip? Bet it is long enough to cover his body if she leaned over him. Riley's mind conjured up a picture of her on top of him, naked breasts jutting out under a curtain of rich brown hair while he pumped into her from below.

"Down boy." He did not need his dick making his decisions for him. Even if that was where most of the blood from his brain was right now.

"—Imperial police are also looking for the captain of this ship," a picture of *The Donegal* was shown. "For questioning regarding his whereabouts on the night the Emperor was captured, as well as anyone who has information on the disappearance of Major Lara McDaniel." The newscaster rattled off the codes for the Imperial police and the news satellite.

What the *feck* had he gotten into? They were trying to pin this on *him*? It was definitely time to wake up the Major. They needed to have a talk before any more shit hit the exhaust.

Riley stomped into his sleeping quarters, not even trying to quiet his steps. He jammed on the light with his hand and pushed the door open without knocking. It was his room and if she didn't want to get rudely awakened then she shouldn't hog the damn bed.

He had taken no more than two steps into the room when Lara pulled her laser from under her pillow, rolled out of the bunk and swept his leg right out from under him. Before he could take a breath he was staring at one furious, naked woman holding a laser on him.

"Uh, time to get up?" Riley didn't move a muscle. He wasn't sure if she was going to use that laser on him or not. Although if he had to die, being shot in the head while looking at a gorgeous, naked woman would be on the top of his list.

Her hands held the laser steady, but that wasn't what caught his complete attention. His new partner had the best-looking set of breasts he'd every clapped eyes on, and he wanted to have a hell of a lot more than eyes on those babies. She had big, brown nipples that made his mouth water, and he had the insane urge to sit up and lick them until she begged for mercy.

He could feel his dick spring to full awareness as he continued his visual journey. Her stomach was sculpted, and her legs went on for ages. Those beauties looked strong enough to wrap around a man and hold him just where she wanted. And oh boy, he knew where he wanted to be. The pressure built at the base of his cock, and the urge to sink himself into her body almost overcame his wariness of the laser she was holding on him. Almost.

"For the love of shooting stars! Would you knock or something first? I could have killed you!" She had the nerve to yell at him.

He didn't think this was the time to remind her that it was his room they were talking about. "Do you mind putting that thing away? Or at least pointing it somewhere else?"

Lara put the laser on the bed and stepped back so he could get up. His blood heated to boiling when he smelled her scent. She didn't seem to realize that she was standing there butt naked. Hey, if she didn't care, he wasn't about to tell her.

"What was so important that you had to wake me up like a herd of *toradals* tromping through?" she asked grabbing her suit off the bed and stepping into it without the least bit of embarrassment. As soon as she slipped her arms in and buttoned the collar, the thing just melded itself to her body. He didn't see a zipper or attachment or anything. Blast, there wasn't even a seam to show where it separated.

"What is that thing?" Riley slowly walked around her, looking at the suit that clung to every curve on her body. It was driving him crazy knowing she had nothing on underneath it. The only thing standing between him and that beautiful body was this paper-thin suit. At this rate he'd have permanent brain damage from lack of oxygen.

"The latest and greatest invention for outfitting the troops. It monitors your vital signs, has a homing signal built in, and it is suited for any environment. It's great except for the fact that it attaches to your body like some kind of alien growth. That took a little getting used to. Now what did you want to tell me?" She arched an eyebrow and crossed her arms over her chest.

Tell her? He wanted to tell her all sorts of stuff. Hell he wanted to *show* her all sorts of stuff. If he had the time he was sure he would have plenty to say... Oh! That's right, they didn't have any time. Shit.

"We are in big trouble."

"What do you mean 'we'?"

"I just saw a newscast about the Emperor's disappearance. Seems that the kidnappers have made no demands, but the sources say all hands on *The Federation* are lost and they are looking into your disappearance. Oh, and they are looking to question me about it."

"What? How could anyone have even known I was missing? If they tried to contact the ship and everyone was dead, they wouldn't know if I was alive or dead."

Her face crumpled a bit and turned an alarming shade of white. Riley was afraid she might do something stupid like cry on him. Hell, he didn't blame her for being upset about losing her crew. He knew how a troop could become family, and this was like losing a whole city. But, *feck*, he didn't want to deal with a woman's tears.

She turned away and gathered her composure for a few minutes before facing him again. Her eyes still looked suspiciously glassy, and her voice was husky, but her gaze was steady. "This doesn't make any sense. How could they know about you? Unless someone saw you pick me up and thought it was very convenient." She strapped her laser to her leg and continued to walk around the room.

Every time she passed by him, he got the unmistakable scent of woman in his brain. He had to force himself not to stare at her chest when she walked towards him, but didn't even try to stop himself from checking out her ass on the return trip.

"Did you send out a distress call when you took off?"

"Of course I did. That's standard procedure."

"So presumably someone could have heard your call and set off to find out what happened, saw the ship and assumed everyone was dead." Riley was having a hard time concentrating, but he thought that made sense.

"That's a possibility, but then how do they know about you?"

"I haven't quite figured that part out yet. I wasn't looking to be in this area, I was just following the scraps."

"Following the scraps? I don't understand."

"I pick up scrap metal and sell it to mineral-poor planets. They melt it down and use it to build things. Big cruisers dump all sorts of junk into space. I haul it in and take what I can use, and recycle the rest. The bigger the ion trail, the bigger the ship. The bigger the ship, the better the chance for a prime haul. I was half-assed following an ion trail on my way to Epsilon to waste a few credits on women and booze when I ran across what I thought was a purge. Only I found you instead."

"I was following the ion trails of the ships that took the Emperor. I went around the dump and never saw what hit me."

"Did you see the ships? Can you describe what they look like?"

"No, I never saw them. By the time I got to a speeder they were long gone. My only hope was to follow the ion trails until I could get some more help."

"So you never got a look at their ships?"

"No, I was trying to stay alive and keep up the chase. I was slightly outnumbered."

"How many men came? What was their formation? What were they wearing?"

Lara closed her eyes and took three deep breaths. She pulled the scene back into her head. She didn't know much about ships, but ground battles were her area of expertise. She'd been preparing for them from the time she was five years old. Eyes still closed she spit out the information he asked like she was giving report.

"Average height, well-trained. They never said a word, didn't need to communicate with one another, each knew their job. Two advance scouts, four rear guards, and four in the main force."

"So that is five, maybe six ships."

"How do you know?"

"What you just described is the standard operating formation for a tag and drag mission of the Traminian Black Operations."

"Really? And how would someone like you know what the most elite forces in Tramin use for standard operating formations?"

"Because I was a squad leader for five years and a scout for ten."

Well, stars. That put a little different spin on things. Lara tried to assimilate this new information while fighting the powerful attraction she was feeling for him. She had been breathing in his scent the whole time she slept, and it had given her some very erotic dreams. Apparently he was more than just another pretty face.

"If you were a squad leader for five years, what are you doing flying around collecting junk for a living in this tub?"

"That's a whole 'nother story, one we don't have time for now. We are in some deep shit, and sinking fast. We need to find out why the government's best unit was sent out to get the Emperor, and how they got the information to take him out so quickly. This reeks of an inside job."

"What was your first clue?" Lara pushed herself away from her corner of the room and brushed past Riley into the main cabin. It really burned her ass that someone she knew, probably trusted, poisoned the crew of *The Federation*. Someone was going to pay for this. As soon as she found the Emperor, she would make sure the culprits were punished not just for kidnapping old Touchy Thomellt, but for endangering her crew. She refused to believe that they were all dead.

"There's no need to get sarcastic here. The way I see it neither one of us is in a good position. You screwed up and lost your Emperor, and looks like the Emeraldians want to blame it on me. The only way out of this is if we get the Emperor back and find out who is behind it."

Lara didn't like hearing that she screwed up from a scruffy space scavenger like Riley, but he had a point. They needed to cooperate to get out of this mess, even if it killed her. "Fine, what's your big plan?" This ought to be interesting. Although she had to admit, she'd take him a little more seriously now that she knew he had some military experience.

"Like I said before, what we need most is information. Since everyone in the whole *fecking* galaxy is looking for this ship, we're going to have to get our information underground."

"Which means what exactly?"

"I was going to go to Epsilon and hit some of the old bars where the Traminian grunts used to hang out, but that isn't possible anymore."

"You're repeating yourself. What is it you are trying to avoid telling me?" Lara did not like the way he wouldn't look at her. She just knew she wasn't going to like what his idea was, but for the life of her she couldn't figure out what he was thinking.

"We're still going to Epsilon, but instead of the main port we're going to one that is for—ah, independent shippers."

"You mean smugglers, don't you?" Did he think she was some sort of prude? "Do you think I'm going to go around trying to bust people? I don't give a *limfa's* ass about who smuggles what from whom, as long as I get the information I need to get the Emperor back I can look the other way."

"It's more than just that."

"Well spit it out!"

"In the areas we are going to, there aren't very many women. And the ones who are there have very specific, ah, positions."

"What do you mean, positions?" She knew she wasn't going to like this. Traminians were famous for their subjection of women. Growing up in military school didn't exactly give her a lot of experience being a meek and mild woman. "Do you mean I'm going to have to stand behind you and keep my eyes down or something like that?"

"Not exactly. In the Traminian underground women are servants, whores, or concubines. The only way I'm going to be able to keep you with me is if you are my concubine."

Chapter Five

A concubine? Lara had heard stories about Traminian concubines since she figured out boys were different from girls. Many of the guys she grew up with thought having a Traminian concubine was the ultimate in carnal pleasure.

Girls were chosen from the poor villages in the hills for their beauty, and taken into special training until they were old enough for sale. After they had been trained sufficiently they were sold at private auctions for huge sums of money, very little of which went to the families who lost their daughters.

Once purchased, the concubines became the property of their owners for life. Her life. They could be bequeathed to descendants like any other asset. As they got older and became less valuable, they assumed other roles in their owner's household, depending on the benevolence of their master. A concubine's life could either be heaven or hell depending on who bought her at the tender age of sixteen.

"You're kidding, right? Why can't I just be a servant? I could suck it up for a few days." Well, she could try anyway.

"No way. A servant wouldn't be allowed to stay with me during dinner or while I was conducting business."

"Oh, and your whore would be?"

"Outside of the house, a concubine is bound to her master, wherever he goes, she goes. That is why you see so very few of them out of the home. For their protection they must always be with their masters so that they can't be stolen away."

"How very gracious of them."

"You could just stay on the ship while I go digging, if you don't think you can play along." Riley leaned back against the wall and shot her a challenging look.

"Right. And I'll just 'trust' you to find the information about the Emperor and not spend your time in the whorehouses on Epsilon. What do I have to do to be a concubine?"

"First you have to stop shooting me daggers with your eyes. Concubines love their masters, or know enough to fake it very well. They're trained from the time they are little girls to please their masters. They give up all will to their owners."

"There is no way I'm going to be able to pull this off." Lara kicked her heel against the wall.

"Fine, I'll go alone. But you'll have to stay locked in the bedroom while I'm gone. I don't trust you not to go off on your own the minute my back is turned."

Since that was exactly what she had in mind, she didn't bother to protest her innocence.

"We won't be there long, if you behave yourself and don't get us into any trouble. You dress like a concubine, walk behind me, say 'yes, master' while I find out what the *feck* is going on, and we're out of there in two hours flat."

"Where are you going to find a costume to fit me? I doubt most concubines are almost six feet tall, and I really doubt that you just happen to have some clothes lying around."

"On that you would be wrong. It just so happens that in one of my hauls, I got an entire trunk of clothes. I'm sure we can piece together something for you. The tough part is going to be finding something that looks close enough to the bindings to pass unnoticed." He was staring at her from his spot by the door. He'd been there since she helped him off the floor. She could feel his eyes burning holes through her uniform, touching her intimately every time her back was turned.

"Bindings?" This was going from bad to worse.

"Yeah, I told you, all concubines are bound to their masters while they are out in public."

"By what?"

"They are bound by a collar around their throats and one around their waists that are connected to their master's waist."

"No sparking way! Forget it! I'll just go down disguised as a man and get my own information. There is no way I am putting a dog collar around my neck for any man."

"Hey, it's your ass on the line, not mine. I can change my identity and ship with a few credits in the right hands. I'll leave you there and go on my way with no worries whatsoever." He crossed his arms over his chest and leaned back against the door. His smug smile wavered a little when his butt hit the doorframe.

Good. Hope his ass is killing him from where he hit the ground.

"*Toradal-shit*. You already told me that you needed to clear your name, and that we should 'cooperate'. What part of this scheme shows your cooperation?"

"I'm the one with the contacts in the underground. I'm also the one who is going to do all the talking while you stand there and distract them. And I promise I won't touch you, or make it harder than it has to be. Come on, Sweet Cheeks, it's only for a couple of hours and then you can put the dog collar on me." He gave her a devastating grin, almost, but not quite melting her resolve.

"You keep your hands to yourself."

"Team honor," he said, crossing his heart. "I'll only touch you enough to keep up pretenses."

"Give me the sparking clothes."

"I knew you could do it. Go get changed and I'll hunt something up for a collar."

"Just one thing, Flyboy."

"Yeah?"

"If we don't get the Emperor back after all of this, your life-span will be counted in minutes."

Lara stormed off towards the bedroom without looking back.

* * * * *

What had she gotten herself into? Lara looked at herself in the mirror, and looked at the picture Riley had given her to help her figure out what went where.

The picture showed a petite woman wearing the silk scarf across her breasts, and the gauze ones layered over her hips as a multicolored skirt. Her feet were bare, and she had a jeweled collar and belt with thin chains connecting them in a line down her exposed stomach.

On Lara, the silk scarf pushed her breasts up to overflowing. There seemed to be a great deal of flesh exposed between the scarf covering her boobs and where the ones around her hips started. She wasn't sure if she had those tied correctly or not. Everything was covered, but when she took a step her leg was exposed practically up to her crotch. There was no way she was bending over in this get-up, that was for sure. Stars, there was no way she could go out in public wearing scraps of silk and gauze.

"Hey, we're almost at Epsilon, you ready yet?"

"Yeah, keep your pants on, I'll be out in a minute."

Lara pulled her braid over her shoulder and laid it over her chest as she walked out the door. If Riley valued his life, he'd better keep his smart-ass comments to himself.

* * * * *

"I think I found something that will work as a collar as long as no one looks too closely. The chances of any of these guys knowing what an actual concubine collar looks like are slim so we should be okay—" Riley trailed off as he caught a look at Lara walking into the main cabin.

He had thought her skintight spacesuit was arousing, but Lara in the scraps of silk that made up a concubine's outfit was devastating. Her breasts were pushed up by the scarf covering them until he was afraid a deep breath would push them completely out. Afraid? He was hoping she would sneeze! The scarves around her hips softened the muscles in her legs, making her look feminine and wanton.

Riley had seen plenty of concubines in the markets on Tramin, but never one as screamingly sensual as Lara. Her body might be honed from years of fighting, but the lush curves and long legs were made for loving, and she didn't even realize it. She stood in front of him looking awkward and uncomfortable, and Riley wanted to do was pull off the skimpy scarf holding her breasts, with his teeth. His cock stood at attention, right in line with his hormones' plan. *Feck*, she'd distract his informants all right. He'd be lucky if he could keep a thought in his own head.

"Uh, here, try this on." Riley didn't trust himself to get close enough to her to put the collar and belt on himself. All that pale flesh was making his hands itch to touch her. His mouth was watering at every curve and dip. He could almost see her nipples pushing through the silk, and he wanted to plant his mouth right there and feast for hours. The pressure of his cock against his pseudo-leather pants was becoming slightly unbearable.

"Is this the latest fashion in slave wear?" She looked uncomfortable and pissed off all at once.

"Think of it as going undercover for a mission, that should help."

"Right. Easy for you to say, you aren't going out in public wearing nothing but scraps of silk."

"No, but your spacesuit shows almost as much."

"It does not! Besides, everyone else on board *The Federation* had to wear one too. It leveled the playing field. Here, I'm going to be dressed as a whore around a bunch of men for all of them to stare at and paw."

"No one will touch you. You have my word on that. Touching someone's concubine is like touching a guy's dick." He really didn't want to think about touching dicks right now. He wanted her to touch his in the worst way.

"Just keep in mind, I am *not* a concubine. No one owns me. And anything you do will come back to haunt you." She looked at him with fire in her dark brown eyes. He didn't doubt her for a second.

Without saying a word, Riley attached the gold chains he had scrounged to a link in the collar and on the belt. The chain snaked down between her breasts and glinted like a river of sunlight against her skin. He took a deep breath before he opened his mouth. He needed all the oxygen he could get.

"I'll protect you from harm. You have my word."

"I'll protect myself, you just get the information as soon as possible and get us out of this mess."

Riley groaned as she turned and stalked off. The skirt was meant for mincing steps, not ground-eating strides, the perfect globes of her ass flashed him with every heart-stopping step.

He had to get his mind out of his pants and back on the situation or he'd be a dead man before he cleared his name. He had been bluffing about not caring about it. Apparently he hadn't bluffed very well because she had seen right through him. Ever since he'd been demoted from Squad Leader, his name, his cat and this ship were the only things he had. It had taken all of his savings, and quite a few favors to get his hands on this ship, he wasn't giving it up without a fight.

Slipping into the captain's chair, Riley charted the course for the backside of Epsilon Station. The main docking bay would be crawling with what passed for Federation officials in this part of space. Luckily his ship came not only with a cloaking device, but some other pretty handy accessories for getting in and out of places unobserved. That was part of the reason it had cost so *fecking* much.

Riley switched on the cloaking device, and bypassed the drones set out to catch anyone who didn't check in at the authorized ports. He searched for the signal that would tell him where the current back door was. It changed somewhat regularly.

Federation officials would come out after they had received too many complaints about smugglers, find the secret entrance and shut it down. They'd hang around looking important for a while in their United Galaxies Federation cruisers, then leave. They wouldn't hit hyperdrive before a new entrance was being made. For enough money, and with the right connections, an independent businessman like Riley could get a device for his ship that identified him as a space scavenger and not a Federation official. The guards in the underground didn't care where he got his cargo, as long as he didn't ask too many questions about where they got the money to buy it.

When he saw the red light on the bottom of the station flash a series of blinks, he slowed down and steered towards the cleverly disguised opening.

"*Feck*, Riley, been a long time since you've been by. Whatcha doin'? Slumming?" A grizzled, one-legged old man appeared on the vid screen.

"Nah, just haven't had much to sell. Decided to come by and see what's going on, things have been a mite boring in space lately." Luckily the snort coming from the bedroom couldn't be heard over the monitor.

"Well, bring her on into bay three. You need a refill while you're here?"

"Nope, don't think I'll be here that long. Just coming in for a quick drink and some conversation."

"Right, and I'm the Emperor." The old man cackled as he turned off the screen.

Riley made sure his monitor was turned off too before he addressed Lara.

"Do you want to blow this whole thing? Do you?"

"Hey, I'm dressing the part, I'm wearing your damn chains, what the hell else do you want from me?"

"I want you to grow up and act the part for two *fecking* hours. All you have to do is pretend to be subservient while we're here. Trust me, after seeing you in action I know you are anything but. Do your job and keep your mouth shut."

"Fine. I'll keep my mouth shut and my eyes lowered, but don't fuck it up or I'll have your balls—"

"Yeah, yeah, I know. You'll have my balls as earrings. Let's go, Sweet Cheeks. The sooner we get out there, the sooner we can leave."

"I swear I'm going to get you for this."

"Yeah, yeah, whatever." Riley didn't bother telling her that there was no way she could torture him any worse than being with her dressed like that and knowing he couldn't touch her. He knew she didn't have perfume with her, yet she smelled sweet and sexy all on her own.

"Don't march, glide. Your sole purpose in life is to please me, not save the world. You are supposed to float along behind me, attentive to my every need. Don't roll your eyes at me, don't snort, and blast it, relax your shoulders. You're a concubine, not a Major, you don't need to stand at attention here you know."

"It's the only way I know how to stand. I've been in the military my whole life. I've had people telling me to stand up straight since I could walk, I can't just slouch now because you order it."

Riley felt a pang in a heart he had long since forgotten he had. There was something wrong with the galaxy when people are telling a five year old to stand at attention.

"Here, take this." He handed her a tablet.

"What is it? An aphrodisiac?"

"No, I don't need those. It's a muscle relaxer. It should help you soften up without knocking you out. It's okay, trust me."

"I really wish you'd stop saying that." Lara popped the pill.

While she was distracted, Riley clipped the end of the chain to his waist, effectively binding her to him. Good thing he had found a long chain, she was damn tall. He saw a glint of rebellion in her eyes, but she suppressed it and squared her shoulders. He sighed.

"Think vixen, seductress," he tried.

"Wimp," she said, but she relaxed her shoulders and her back into a gentle sway.

"Whatever works. It's showtime!"

They walked down the ramp to the filthy landing bay. Riley thought about Lara's bare feet and winced. Who knew what she would stop on or in. He stopped short, turned, and lifted her into his arms.

"What are you doing?" Lara whispered in his ear, gripping his shoulders like a safety bar.

"This floor is full of crap, literally and figuratively. Dirty, bleeding feet aren't exactly attractive." He liked the feel of her in his arms. Her breasts rubbed against his chest, and his arm cradled her almost bare ass. Her skin was baby soft, and getting warmer by the minute. He could see her pupils dilating, and her breath started to come a little more rapidly. *Feck*, he could even smell her desire. Riley tried not to think that the only thing separating him from her pussy was a thin scrap of silk inches from his mouth.

Still, he couldn't help but glance down at the shadowed cleft between her legs. Lara's breathing hitched and she squirmed a bit in his arms.

Good, he wasn't going to be the only one suffering.

"Whatcha got there, Riley?" The grizzled codger craned his head to see more of Lara's legs.

"I got me a concubine from a new lordling who couldn't handle her. We traded a bit and I don't know who got the better end of the bargain."

"Tehee! Looks like you got your hands full!" He slapped his knee at his own wit.

Riley groaned silently. He could feel Lara tense up and gave her side a warning squeeze. "Is the *One-Eyed Snake* still open? Or have the Feds closed it again?"

"Nope, it's still open, but why you'd want to go to a place like that when you got yourself your own bunny there, I don't know."

"Gotta have a little variety you know. Have her ready to go in a hurry, Mac, just in case."

"Always do, Riley, always do. You haven't left this station yet when you wasn't on the run."

"Makes life more interesting that way," he shot over his shoulder as he walked through the reeking filth on his way to the bar.

"What is that stench? It smells like a sewage tank," Lara whispered in his ear.

"Probably was. I'll bet they rerouted at least one pipe to open this place up. Must have hit a line in the process."

"Why don't they clean it up?"

"Maybe because the stink will keep the authorities away longer."

"Better get me a pair of boots in case we have to make a run for it. Running through that in bare feet is a good way to get blood poisoning."

"Don't worry, I'll take care of it."

"I can't tell you how that relieves me."

"Remember meek, submissive? Not sarcastic."

"No one is around right now; I don't have to keep up the act." He noticed she looked around anyway.

Riley let her slide down his body when they reached the outside corridor. Someone had left a cleaning unit humming outside the door. Probably so no one left a trail of shit to their hiding place. He didn't much care, as long as he got the filth off his boots. Taking a minute to get his bearings, Riley surveyed the area.

Several lights were out in this section of the Station. The inhabitants of these parts preferred the cover of darkness for their dealings. Riley looked at Lara to make sure she wasn't casing the joint like a soldier, and almost ruined everything by snorting out loud.

Lara had the glazed expression of a *toradal* cow in love. She was staring at him with a saccharine look of adoration on her face, her shoulders relaxed, and her hips thrust out. The end of her braid was clasped in her hands and she looked at him like he was the suns, moons, and stars all tied up in a bow for her.

"Come on, Bunny, I've got a man to talk to about a ship." Riley snickered to himself at the common nickname for a concubine. He was sure she was burning up inside at all the liberties he was taking, but hell, it was fun watching her pretend to be docile. "Don't lay it on too thick," he whispered as he pulled her close to his side. She fit his frame like a hand in a glove. He didn't have to lean down to touch her, and her ear was just the right height for exploration. Seeing a golden opportunity, he nipped her tempting earlobe and felt her shiver.

"Same goes. You don't need to be pawing me in public do you?"

"Better get used to it. You're my prized possession, and I like to play with my toys."

"I will get even, you know," she told him while maintaining the empty-headed expression on her face. He'd love to know how she could look at him like he was a vid star while issuing threats at the same time.

"Looking forward to it. Now behave, here's the Snake. Don't say a word, but keep your eyes open. Tug on the chain if you see something I should know about. And stay away from mirrors and windows."

"I can see the windows, but why mirrors?"

"That's were the lasers are hidden. If Sly sees something suspicious, he fires first and asks questions later. I don't want to get hit in the crossfire if I can avoid it."

"Great."

"Two hours, Sweet Cheeks, just two hours and we'll be on our way."

"You'd better be right," she growled while nuzzling his neck.

He really hoped he was.

Chapter Six

Lara almost gagged at the smell of booze, smoke, and unwashed bodies. With all the technological advances over the centuries she still couldn't understand why science couldn't develop cure for body odor. Riley pulled her towards a table in the rear of the crowded bar. She had to force herself to keep her eyes only on him. Her back itched with the feeling of hundreds of eyes crawling over her body.

This had better work. Riley sat down and pulled her onto his lap. He ordered a syntho-beer from the wait-screen next to him and pretended to fondle her as he waited for its arrival.

"What are you doing?" she hissed into his ear, playing with his chest hair. He was wearing skintight pseudo-leather pants and a white shirt that was open at the top. He looked sexier than any man had a right to under the circumstances.

"I'm waiting until someone comes to me. If I go around asking the questions this place will clam up and I'll never find anything out. And stop wiggling on my lap."

"What's wrong? Game not so much fun anymore?" She trailed her tongue around the shell of his ear and slipped her hand into the loose shirt to play with his flat male nipple. Let's see how he liked being pawed in a public place. "I'm just playing my part. Doing my best to please my master." She wiggled some more against the erection poking her in the ass. Was it getting hot in here? The pill he had given her had left her feeling loose-limbed and relaxed, maybe it was making her feel hot and breathless, too.

"Please me much more and we won't get any information." His head was thrown back and the veins in his neck were throbbing. She wanted to stick her mouth right there and suck in that beating pulse. The urge to touch his cock was overwhelming. His hand tightened on the bare skin of her waist, and his other hand climbed up her thigh, sending flames straight to her pussy.

"Stop looking at me like that."

"And how is that, Master?" She couldn't stop looking at the veins on his neck. His green eyes were so brilliant, like the stones on her home planet, Emeraldia. His sandy hair kept flopping into his eyes and she moved it away without thinking. The innocent contact sent a laser beam through her system, incinerating every brain cell she had.

"Like you want to eat me alive," he whispered, bringing his hand up to cup her cheek.

"Isn't that how I'm supposed to look?" She could barely get the words out; her throat seemed to be thick with an emotion she couldn't name. Her breath caught in her throat as he pulled her closer to his mouth. She licked her lips in anticipation as his breath mingled with her own.

"Riley! You old space pirate! How the hell are you?" A man the size of Lara's first drill sergeant spun a chair around and straddled it. She was surprised when the chair didn't break underneath his massive frame. He had wildly curling red hair and a full beard that reminded her of a moving bush on his face.

"Hey, Dolf, long time no see." Riley continued to fondle her, but the tension was broken.

She didn't know if she should thank this Dolf or hate him.

"So what brings you to this part of the galaxy? Got something for sale?" He eyed her exposed flesh like she was the last candy bar on the shelf.

"Maybe, maybe not. You know anyone interested in buying anything?"

"Always someone buying or selling something around here."

Lara listened to their conversation with only a small part of her brain. She knew enough to let Riley deal with his cronies without her interference. She played with the buttons on his chest and scanned the room while pretending to nuzzle Riley's neck. A part of her heated up at the pure male smell coming from his skin, she really, really wanted to taste him all over. The feel of his cock pressed against her was making her pussy so wet she'd be lucky if the scrap of silk she was wearing didn't get soaked right through.

Focus! Just because she was pretending to be a sex slave didn't mean she had to think like one. Stars, almost thirty years of discipline down the tubes after a day with a space pirate. She really hoped this little escapade didn't get back to High Command.

Pulling herself together, she pushed the carnal thoughts out of her mind and looked around for anyone who might look familiar, or set off her internal alarms. Most of the patrons had a harsh, bitter look to them. This was the garbage purge of the galaxy. The very people she'd always thought she'd have to save her Emperor from, and instead she was looking to them for help.

Not help, she corrected, just information. She did not need the help of the great unwashed to do her job, damn it. Riley squeezed her again in warning and she pulled her attention back to the giant of a man sitting across from them. As she turned, she caught someone staring at her out of the corner of her eye. She cringed at the thought of another set of eyes crawling all over her, then realized he wasn't looking at her that way.

This pair of eyes was looking at her with loathing. Shit, a very familiar loathing. What was his name? Lara searched her memory for how she knew those cold blue eyes raking her over the coals. She pulled on the chain and nudged Riley's cheek with her nose.

"Ten o'clock, I know that guy. Can't place him right now, but it can't be good the way he's staring at me," she cooed into his ear and giggled like an airhead. Shit, he was walking towards their table. "Time to get out of here." It was hard to act like you were seducing someone when you really just wanted him to get his ass in gear.

"Thanks for the information, but looks like I've been ignoring Bunny here for too long. Think I'll get myself a room for a few hours and then head out." Too late, the guy was already at the table, blocking them in.

"You can't go so soon. We haven't even seen your slave dance." Dolf hadn't moved his bulk yet, so they couldn't get out that way either. This was not good.

"She's not for public entertainment. I don't like to share."

"My friends here and I think you should. None of us have ever seen a concubine dance before. I hear they got moves that will turn a man's knees to water."

"You couldn't handle her moves, buddy."

Lara had never taken a dancing lesson. She'd taken karate and other martial arts training for years, but the military didn't send its orphans to dancing school. She couldn't dance a step to save her life.

Looked like she was going to have to try.

"I betcha she isn't even a real concubine, boys. I think Riley is trying to pull a fast one on us." The room started to rumble with displeasure.

Lara didn't like their odds of getting out of there alive. Spark it, she knew this guy, and she would bet her last credit he knew her too. He turned to goad the crowd a little more and it hit her. She had arrested him for beating the snot out of one of the working girls back home. He was a mean son of a bitch, and by arresting him she had saved him from getting pulverized by the rest of the troop. The woman he had beaten almost to death was the favorite prostitute of the troop at the time. Lara had saved his foul life. Apparently he didn't thank her for it.

The rumblings of the crowd were getting louder, she could see Riley pleading for her to stay calm. There was no way she was going to be able to fight her way out of here, but maybe she could bluff her way out.

"If it pleases my master, I will dance for his friends' enjoyment." Idiot, he almost blew it by looking at her like she had two heads. "Can I pick the music?"

Men stumbled all over themselves to make room for her to pick something out on the music player. Riley walked with her, as the chain didn't leave him much choice in the matter.

"Have you ever danced before?" he whispered into her ear.

"Not a step," she whispered back, trying to find something she could work with on the player.

"Then what the *feck* are you trying to do? Get us killed? These guys are expecting a striptease, what are you going to do? March around?"

"I'll think of something, you just keep an eye on the ringleader there. I busted him once and I think he's out for revenge."

"Great, just great."

"You guys picking out music or playing slap and tickle? Get a move on here, we want some entertainment!"

"I'll worry about dancing; you worry about getting us out of here once I'm done. I have a feeling that Rat Face isn't going to let us out of here without a fight."

Lara didn't recognize any of the music, so she picked a song at random and stepped to the middle of the room with Riley in tow.

"First a few ground rules, boys," Riley said as he pulled a laser out of his belt. "Bunny is my concubine, and the hand that touches her will be twitching on the floor ten seconds later. This is a rare treat for you slobs, don't screw it up. Now move those tables back and make some room. And remember, I'm watching you like a Fed at roundup." Riley unclasped the chain from his belt without taking his eyes off the crowd. No one appeared to doubt the seriousness of his words.

Lara took a deep breath and let the music throb through her as an impromptu dance floor was cleared for her. She could feel Riley move behind her for a minute, then move away. She shivered without his bulk to warm her. Men gathered around the space on benches and chairs, all waiting for her to begin. Stars above, how was she going to pull this off?

Hmm, pull this off. Maybe that was the key.

Taking one of the scarves from around her waist, Lara slid it through her hands until it was pulled tight. Rolling her hips as best she could, she ran the scarf between her breasts and around them, pushing them up higher. Whistles and catcalls filled the air as the globes threatened to pop right out of their bindings.

The music was pulsing in her brain, making her move to the beat despite her lack of grace. The men didn't have a clue whether she could dance or not, all they knew was that her breasts were big, and her skirt was practically see-through. Their mouths were slack, and their eyes never left her as she used the scarf to test the force of gravity.

Lara was used to having power over men, but this was control of a totally different kind. And damn if she wasn't enjoying it. She tossed the scarf up into the air and leaned back to catch it, thrusting her hips out and practically exposing her mound. Trailing her hand down her body, she fluttered the scarves that concealed her pussy from the crowd. Before anyone could get a glimpse, she spun around, her braid flying out behind her. Lara bent over in front of Riley who was standing by the door with his arms over his chest. He looked pissed off, and more than a little excited.

Good.

Moving closer to him, hips rolling like a speedster in turbulence, she pushed him down into a chair. It wasn't hard. He sat down heavily, like a man in a trance. His eyes never left hers, until she bent over and put her hands on his thighs. His muscles were rock-hard and flexed under her fingers.

Using her arms, Lara pushed the sides of her boobs in, until they were double their normal size and practically under her chin. Looking right into his green eyes, she slowly bent her head and licked her own breasts.

She could actually feel his cock grow under his pants, and she wasn't even touching it. Sending him a wicked grin and a wink, she turned around and bent over, giving him a view of her ass, which was wiggling practically in his face. The dancing was making her hot, both physically and sexually. She could feel her cleft growing and swelling as she moved to the beat. Her pussy lips were so big and wet every movement sent jolts of sensation surging through her. She felt sexy and powerful, and in complete control of the room full of men.

Caught up in the game, Lara jumped when she felt a sharp slap on her butt. Twirling around, she gave the room quite a view of her legs before she faced Riley. He sat there smirking at her. Oh yeah? Take this!

Lara climbed on top of his lap, still gyrating to the music. Wrapping the scarf around his neck, she pulled him into her breasts for the barest of seconds, then pushed him back. Bending over backwards, she continued wiggling against him. Her mound was pressed right against his erection, and sent her already heightened senses soaring.

The only noise in the room was the dying beat of the music. Lara trailed her hand between her breasts and down her stomach before pulling herself up against Riley again. Drawing his head to her heaving chest, she felt her pussy lips swell even more. The feel of his breath blowing over her barely covered nipples stimulated them to hard little nubs. His eyes were blazing hot and stared into hers with a promise she couldn't read. Her body was on fire for his, and didn't give a damn that this was only supposed to be pretend. There was nothing fake about the storm about to erupt in her body.

* * * * *

Riley grabbed her face and dragged her down in a flaming hot kiss. The music died completely, and there was only the sound of his mouth on Lara's for endless seconds. Finally, cheers and shouts went up, breaking the spell that had wound around them.

"Satisfied?" Riley asked Rat Face, standing up. He hooked the chain back on Lara and pulled her behind him. Looking around the room he noticed he wasn't the only one sporting a hard-on the size of a cargo flyer. Was he going to have to fight his way out of here just to keep Lara to himself? Did he want Lara to himself? His dick slammed painfully in his pants. *Guess that answers that question.*

"No. None of us have ever seen a concubine dance, how do we know for sure that was really a dance?" Rat Face seemed to be the only one who hadn't fallen under Lara's spell.

Blast, this guy really was out for trouble. "Look around you, man, every dick in this place is standing at attention, what more proof do you need? What do you want from us anyway? You want me to fuck her right here?" As soon as the words were out of his mouth he knew he was in trouble. Man, open mouth insert foot.

"Nice going, Flyboy," Lara muttered just loud enough for him to hear.

Rat Face had a satisfied smile cross his features. Shit, he'd stepped right into an ambush.

"Now that you mention it, I think that sounds like a fine idea. Don't you boys?"

Feet stomped and mugs were raised overhead as the crowd scented a new game.

"Wait just a *fecking* minute here. I don't care what you want; I am not having sex in front of you. I doubt I could even get it up with you all staring and critiquing my performance." Right, like just the idea of sinking into her hot body wasn't enough to keep him hard for days.

"If you can't get it up I sure can!" came a call from the crowd.

"Like hell. I don't care if I have to shoot the lot of you; no one is touching my woman!"

Here we go. Riley felt Lara tense behind him, she was preparing herself for a fight.

"I don't think we need to go that far. There's a room right behind the bar there, we can set you up nice and cozy like. Give you a little privacy for your delicate sensibilities." Rat Face was clearly enjoying himself. What was his game? Did he want to expose them, or was he just stalling?

"That defeats the purpose then, doesn't it?"

"We'll still be able to hear the two of you go at it. After the way she dry-fucked you, I'd think you'd be a little more appreciative of my offer." Rat Face looked very pleased with himself. Riley longed to wipe that smug little grin off his face. Too bad thirty or so of his buddies would jump in to rescue him.

Lara nudged him in the shoulder. He hoped she had a plan, because he was running a little low on ideas.

"Come on, Bunny, let's show these *toradal-butts* what they're missing."

They were escorted to a back room by a gauntlet of leering men. Riley's hand hovered near his laser just in case anyone got a dose of bravery and tried to grab Lara. Rat Face pushed them into the room and shut the door behind them. Riley locked the door to the sound of riotous laughter.

"Make sure you scream really loud, Bunny. We all want to know if Riley is as good as he says he is. And you're not getting out of here without giving us what we want." More laughter trailed off, and Riley could hear calls for beer. He could use a drink himself right about now.

Lara had undone the chain and was searching the room for listening devices and monitors. Riley watched her crawl under the bed without fear of what might be growing under there. Her ass was pointed straight up in the air, and the scarves provided very little cover. He ached to grab her hips and sink his cock into her pussy with her in just that position.

"Oh, Master, take me now. I can wait no longer!" Lara motioned him towards the bed, as she jumped on it, making the headboard thump and the mattress squeak.

Somehow he didn't think she was really looking for a tumble with him. Too bad, the bouncing of the mattress made her tits bob up and down like ripe *Emer-melons*. Riley crossed the room and joined her on the bed. In a surprise move, she pushed him on his back and straddled him. He liked a woman who took the initiative. Running his hands up her sides, he grazed her breasts with his thumbs, and was rewarded with a flick of her fingers on his ear.

"Cut the crap, Flyboy, this is no time to get cute," she growled in his ear as she bounced some more on the bed.

"Trust me, I'm not thinking cute thoughts. What's the plan?"

"What do you mean? Don't you have a plan?"

He couldn't think of anything other than the feel of her skin against his hands, and the feel of her center rubbing against his pants. He had never hated an article of clothing as much as he hated those pants right now. "You're the one who told me you could dance. I thought you had a plan."

"It was your idea for me to dress up in this ridiculous outfit."

That ridiculous outfit was driving him mad. He could feel the weight of her impressive chest on him, tempting him to see if it tasted as good as he thought. How was he supposed to think under these conditions? He had to concentrate on something other than releasing the need that was driving him. What did she say again? Oh yeah, she was blaming him for the mess they were in.

"It doesn't matter whose fault it is, we need to think up some way to get out of here. I know where the Emperor might be, but that information isn't going to do us much good if Rat Face doesn't let us out."

"Tell me something I don't know."

"If you keep bouncing like that I'm going to come in my pants."

She stopped immediately and let out a screaming moan like a herd of *limfas* in heat.

Cheers rose from the other room.

"More! More!" she shouted, bouncing harder.

"Lara, you're playing with fire." The scarf covering her breasts wasn't meant for such vigorous exercise and was slipping inch by torturous inch. He could see the tops of her nipples and his mouth watered.

"Listen, I'm doing what I can to get us out of here, you can help or you can complain."

"Fine, I'll do my part." Riley flipped her over onto her back, pushing his thighs between her nearly naked ones. Her mouth opened in an O of shock. He took that as an invitation and swooped in to kiss the breath out of her.

Riley trailed kisses down her throat to the maddening piece of silk that hid her bounty. Using his teeth, he pulled it down the final inches until her luscious breasts sprang free for his demands. Cupping them in the palms of his hands, he pushed the creamy orbs together until he could lick and suck both of her nipples easily.

When he sucked one into his mouth, Lara's hips thrust up and her hands clamped on his head, holding him in place. He ground his still covered dick into her cleft and felt her wetness through his pants. He had to taste her!

Working his way down, he licked and sucked her creamy skin until he reached the scarves around her waist. He was about to nuzzle them apart when there was a crash against the door.

"It's awfully quiet in there!"

"Our mouths are a little busy right now," Riley shouted, trying to go back to his pursuits. Lara kneed him in the shoulder and rolled away, making the bed squeak even more.

"I am not fucking you with an audience." Lara brushed loose tendrils of hair away from her face and glared at him from across the bed. Her pupils were dilated and her chest heaved with her breathing.

Did that mean she'd fuck him if they were alone? He had to get his brain out of his pants! "Just trying to make it as realistic as possible. Unlike you, what the hell was that shriek?"

"It was supposed to be an orgasm."

"Not like any I've heard, and believe me, I've heard plenty."

"Well, I've never had a screaming orgasm; I was doing the best I could. Can we get back to the plan now?"

The plan, the plan. They really did need a plan.

"If we stay in here long enough, do you think they'll get bored and leave?" Lara bit her lip.

"I doubt it. This is the best entertainment they've had in years."

"That's what I was afraid of. What if I go to the door and tell them that I want one of them because I fucked you to death?"

"They wouldn't believe you." There was no *fecking* way he was letting it get around the galaxy that he got fucked to death, even if it was only a trick. "I got it. Go to the door and tell them you want a threesome, they'll fight each other and give us better odds."

She didn't look too enthused by his suggestion.

"Come on, trust me. They'll fall all over each other just to see your tits. By the time they are done ripping each other to shreds, we'll be able to take care of what is left over."

"Why would they believe that?"

"We could say I want a threesome." Just the thought of some other man touching her made him furious though.

"Is that usual for you? I mean have you ever had a, you know, ah—"

"Ménage a trois? Not with another guy I haven't."

"Then why are they going to believe you are suddenly into sex games?"

"We'll make them believe it."

"How are we going to do that?"

Riley thought for a minute, then a plan popped into his mind as his dick slammed even harder against his pants. This might not work, but it sure as hell would be fun trying.

"Here, lay down across my lap and when I spank you, make sure you yell." The thought of Lara over his lap with that sweet ass of hers open to his gaze was almost his undoing. If her look hadn't been enough to freeze his blood he'd have come on the spot.

"You have got to be kidding. There is no way, no way in sparking hell I'm going to let you spank me."

Before he could answer her there was the thud of a shoulder hitting the door.

"Come on, we don't have time for this, come here!"

Riley dragged her to the bed, sat down, and flipped her onto his lap. The silk scarves parted to reveal the white globes of her ass and his heart lurched at the sight.

"Remember, I'm only doing this to get us out of here, I'm getting no satisfaction out of this whatsoever." *Yeah, right.* "And don't forget to scream."

"Screaming isn't going to be a problem," Lara growled.

* * * * *

Lara was so mad her head was about to explode. The fact that she was so hot her pussy was about to self-combust was another matter entirely. She was face down staring at a disgusting floor while her ass was exposed to Riley and his cock was so sparking hard she could feel it against her hip.

She had absolutely no leverage in this position, and the helplessness of it was doing strange things to her insides. After a lifetime in the military, helplessness was unexplored territory. Before she could think about why being out of control could make her feel so hungry, Riley's hand came down with a resounding smack on her butt cheek.

"Ouch!" Lara shouted before she could stop herself.

"Not ouch, you're supposed to like it. It's supposed to get you hot." Riley stroked the area he just slapped.

His other hand was resting on her thigh sending flickers of flame to her pussy. She was getting hot all right.

"People really enjoy this?" She was glad her face was hidden by her position so he couldn't see the truth on her face.

"I don't give a *feck* what other people like, we're putting on a show for an audience here, so sound like you like it."

Riley slapped her again, this time on the other cheek. Stinging pain radiated from where his hand met bare flesh. Warmth followed on the heels of the pain, tingling trails of heat spreading straight to her center. Lara's pussy dripped even more than when his mouth had been on her breasts.

"Come on, scream for them, Sweet Cheeks." Riley said, slapping her again.

Lara let out a shriek, but whether it was from rage or frustration she didn't know. His fingers had somehow slid closer to her crotch and were now mere inches away from her clit. Torturously few inches away.

"That's right, baby. Again."

Riley gave her two more open-handed slaps that echoed off the walls of the room, and Lara screamed with each one. His cock was pressing into her side, and she could feel his labored breathing even as she struggled to control her own. When Riley spanked her again, then thrust a finger inside her pussy her final shriek wasn't from pain but from bone-deep sexual frustration. If he didn't touch her clit soon she'd explode!

"What ya' doin' in there, Riley? You need some cuffs to keep her to the bed?" Raucous laughter thundered on the other side of the door, reminding Lara why she was there. And it wasn't to get off on kinky sex games with Riley.

"I think they'll believe you now. Let me up."

Lara was sweating from need, but she pushed it aside. She had to focus on getting them out of there, and if they made it out alive then she could see about easing this ache Riley created.

Helping her to her feet, Riley held onto her arm as she moved towards the door. His intense green eyes stared into hers for a heart-stopping minute before he shook his head and let her go.

"Make them believe you're desperate for a man between your legs," he finally said.

That shouldn't be too hard.

Chapter Seven

Lara took a deep breath. It didn't help any. She crossed to the door on shaky knees; things were getting way out of control. What was wrong with her? She wasn't supposed to *like* dressing like a tart and being fondled by some halfwit Flyboy. Especially when they were doing it with a roomful of drunk listeners nearby. This was definitely not part of the plan. Closing her eyes, she concentrated on the mission. She had to pull this off. The Emperor's life, *her* life was at stake. Two more deep breaths and she was back in control.

Opening the door a crack, she peeked out to get a feel for the room. The crowd still looked much too big for her liking. They needed to even the odds a little bit. Lara looked back at Riley. He was lying back on the bed with his hands behind his head. Well, didn't he look comfy?

Lara loosely draped the scarf in front of her breasts, and used her arms to push them up higher. She didn't understand the fascination with mammary glands, but she would use whatever weapons she had.

"Excuse me gentleman," Lara strolled into the room just in front of the door. She hoped she looked well fucked. "My master wishes to have one of you join us. Who would like to help me show my master how I pleasure others?" She put on her most bubble-headed expression.

There was a minute of dead silence, and Lara felt sweat drip down her spine. She let the scarf slip a little so that more of her breasts showed. Crap, what if they didn't want to have sex with a six-foot Amazon? Lara was about to drop the scarf completely when there was a rush for the bedroom door.

Men scrambled over each other to get to her. Bodies were flying every which way as the front-runners pushed towards the door and the slower folks pulled them back. Lara waited impatiently for the fists to start flying. Hopefully they would start fighting before they got to her and she was crushed under a pile of unwashed bodies.

One drunken sot was pushed to the ground, fell more likely, and pulled two others down with him. He no sooner staggered to his feet when he was dropped again by a punch from one of the men who broke his fall.

After that, all hell broke loose. Lara moved closer to the door of the bar in readiness. She noticed Rat Face hadn't joined in the melee; he was across the mob of writhing bodies staring at her with open hatred. The urge to flip him a one-fingered salute was hard to resist but she did.

Chairs were starting to fly, and several combatants were limping their way out the door when Riley came up behind her.

"Here, try these on, I found them in the room." He handed her a pair of black boots that had definitely seen better days as he surveyed the room. "Good work, looks like there are only two left standing besides Rat Face. Guess he didn't think your charms were worth fighting for."

"He'd rather fight for the chance to kill me I imagine." Lara didn't even want to think about who the past owner of the boots was, or what diseases he had. They were going to have to make a run for it, and what was coating the boots couldn't be any worse than running through raw sewage.

"Can you run in them?"

"They're a little loose, but I'll manage."

"Good, because if I don't miss my guess, that's a messenger drone coming in and he's headed straight for Rat Face. Let's get out of here."

Lara tied the scarf around her chest the best she could and followed Riley as they made their way to the door. They were almost home free when Rat Face spotted them.

"Stop them! They're Emeraldian spies!"

Riley grabbed her wrist and pulled her down the nearest alley. They tore past lounging prostitutes and scheming johns. No one even bothered to try to stop them. As they tore around the corner, a Traminian soldier pulled his laser on them and fired. Diving behind a reeking garbage receptacle, Riley returned fire, automatically pushing Lara under him.

"You got another laser?" Damned if she was going to sit there like a damsel in distress.

"In my boot," he shouted as he stood up to fire again.

Lara patted his leg down looking for the laser. Her shoulder grazed the inside of his thigh and she felt his penis jump.

"Keep you mind on the guy with the laser, not your crotch!"

"It has a mind of its own. Did you get the *fecking* laser yet or are you too busy feeling me up?"

Finding the tiny weapon, Lara pulled it out and guarded Riley's back. Rat Face would be coming around the corner any minute if he were bright enough to see starshine. She looked over her shoulder to see how Flyboy was doing. His face had the blank look of concentration she recognized as a professional fighter. He was in a zone.

She was still waiting for Rat Face to make his appearance when Riley ducked down and waited. What in the stars was he waiting for?

Suddenly he leaped up and fired. "Run!"

Lara sprinted past the twitching body of the guard without a backward glance. "Do you know where we are?" She had no idea what direction they were headed in after all the twists and turns they had taken. If they got separated she was in major trouble.

"Sort of," he said, not slowing down.

"Sort of! What do you mean 'sort of'?"

"Shut up and save your breath for running."

Her snappy comeback was cut off by a laser shot over their heads. Lara's shot flared wildly while they ran down yet another alley.

"Hurry up and take him out, the bay is down here and I don't want to be watching my ass while we power up."

"Sure, I'll just stop and take aim." Lara cursed at him under her breath. "Keep going, I'll catch up."

Lara dropped back while Riley ran ahead. She set the laser to full stun and waited, finding her center and going into the zone. It was Rat Face who rounded the corner, running full tilt. He had enough time to see Riley was all by himself before Lara took him out with the laser.

"Bastard. I should have let the guys have you on Emeraldia."

"You going to gloat or do you want to get the hell out of here?" Riley called from a doorway. By the stench they must have found the hanger.

"I'm coming! Keep your pants on."

Riley flashed her an evil grin and ran on ahead, fiddling with something in his pocket. Maybe she wouldn't mind too much if he didn't keep his pants on? The view of his tight ass and muscular thighs pumping as he ran down the alley was enough to leave her breathless, if all the running didn't. An image of him lying on top of her, thrusting his hips as she held onto that ass flashed into her brain, sending her hormones soaring.

What was wrong with her? Must be the adrenaline. She'd heard some of the guys say it was the biggest aphrodisiac of all. That must be it; she certainly couldn't find Riley attractive.

Lara ran through the slop on the ground trying to breathe as shallowly as possible through her mouth. Thank the stars the boots came high up on her legs or the muck would be splashing on her. Slamming into the back of Riley's suddenly still body, she realized being covered in shit was the least of her worries. Riley was hiding behind a pile of transport crates, looking at something around the side of them. Three goons were standing in the docking bay in front of the ramp to *The Donegal*. Great.

"What do we do now?" Lara asked him, pulling the laser out.

"Put that back! If you shoot that thing into the bay you could puncture a hole in the ship. That's all we need."

"I had it on stun, I'm not an idiot."

"With the amount of fuel spilled around, all it would take is a spark to set this place up in flames. How are you at hand-to-hand combat, Sweet Cheeks?"

"Keep calling me Sweet Cheeks and you'll find out firsthand. Let's go before the reinforcements get here." She'd had about enough of this subservient crap. She was no slave, and she was certainly no damsel in distress. Slipping the laser in the back of his pants, she strolled towards the waiting thugs. She could hear Riley hissing at her to get back but she ignored him. It was time to do things her way for a change.

"Hey boys, whatcha doin'?" Lara did her best to appear unthreatening and helpless until the first one got in striking distance.

The first schmo hitched up his pants and walked towards her with a decidedly evil gleam in his eye. Lara didn't even give him a chance to defend himself, she wheeled a crescent kick alongside his head and followed it with a chop to his throat. She held back enough so that she didn't collapse his windpipe, but he wasn't going to be getting up again any time soon.

The other two goons ran towards her, pulling knives out of their boots. What was Riley waiting for? An invitation? "Any time you're ready to join the party, Flyboy!" Lara faced off against the first man, hoping Riley would watch her back.

This guy was used to using his size to fight for him. He had very little skill, but a whole lot of bulk. His arms were easily as wide as her thighs. He circled around her, looking for an opening she wasn't going to give him. Lara feinted to the right, hoping he'd take the bait.

He lunged towards her leaving his center wide open and putting himself off balance. Amateur. Lara turned the best spinning sidekick of her life. It was a beautiful thing to behold, but it did no more than make him grunt and stumble.

Damn.

She hoped Riley was doing better than she was, but she didn't dare look over to find out.

The goon shot her a smug grin and came at her arms spread wide. If he got those tree trunks around her, she was dead meat. He was trying to back her into a corner so he could pick her up and squeeze the life out of her. She didn't have time for a wrestling match; she had to take him out in a hurry.

Taking a few steps back to make it look as if his plan was working, Lara got a running start and aimed a flying kick at his knees. It didn't matter how strong he was, knees were a weak point for everyone. She made contact with a satisfying crunch. That should have been the end of it.

Too bad it wasn't.

The goon stumbled up with a roar of rage. Great, all she did was piss him off, now what? His meaty fists were flailing at her head, and she had to bob and weave to keep from getting concussed by them. One hand managed to graze her chin when she wasn't fast enough. Lara tasted blood as she bit down on her tongue and her head exploded with pain.

She had to do something, or he was going to take her down with a lucky swipe. He was guarding his knee now, recognizing her strategy. Faking a kick to his knee, she used his pain against him and slammed the kick between his legs. Stars, she loved flip kicks, they worked every time.

His mouth dropped open and a high-pitched keening came out. He dropped to the floor with a thud, his hands clutching his groin as he coughed and choked.

* * * * *

Riley's balls drew up inside his body as he caught a glimpse at Lara's handling of the thug. He was glad the coast was clear, but that just had to hurt.

"Come on!" Lara gestured imperiously to him.

"I was just waiting for you. What took you so long?" Riley knew he was playing with fire, but damn it was worth it. Her hair was disheveled, and her brown eyes were blazing at him. She was like an Amazon in a vid, magnificent and deadly. His blood was racing, his life was in danger, and he wanted nothing more than to press her up against the nearest wall and plunge inside of her.

"Fire up, Bonny! We need to get out of here now." Riley flipped switches even as he shucked off his boots and scrambled to the pilot's seat. He looked over with surprise when Lara plopped down in the seat next to him and slipped on the headgear.

"What do you have for firepower on this thing?"

"I have plenty of firepower, don't you worry. The switch on the left is for the guns, and the one on the floor over here is for the cannon. Now be quiet so I can concentrate on Max."

"The cat? Don't you think we should be concentrating on getting out of here and getting to the Emperor?"

"The cat is going to tell us if we are headed into a trap or not." Riley dropped the twenty pounds of feline in Lara's lap. "If the hair on his back starts to stand up, let me know."

Riley hit the signal that should open the door. Nothing happened. "Shit! The bastards changed the signal to the door!"

"So how are we getting out of here?"

"Well make our own *fecking* door. Full power, Bonny, we're blasting our way out of here!"

"I thought you said if there was so much as a spark this whole place could blow?"

"Yup. Maybe they should have thought of that before they tried to lock me in here." The whine of the engine was music to his ears, Bonny was almost ready, a few seconds more and they'd be ready.

"Power up complete. Five seconds until arsenal is fully functioning. Four, three, two—"

"Troops are in the hanger!" Lara shouted.

"Let'er have it Bonny!"

Riley fired a cannon at the door and didn't even wait for the flames to dissipate before he pushed his way through them. Fire couldn't survive without oxygen, and there was no oxygen in space.

There was plenty still left in the hanger though. He hit the turbo thrusters and took off as fast as he could. The shock waves from the explosion were enough to shake the ship, but not enough to stop them.

Unfortunately, it wasn't enough to stop the Traminian squadron that was hiding behind a nearby satellite either.

"The cat's hair is up!" Lara told him unnecessarily.

"No kidding, we've got an entire squadron on our tail. I'll handle the front guns, you go take the rear."

Lara scrambled out of the chair without a word. He was grateful for her unusual silence; he really needed to concentrate on keeping them in one piece.

"I'm in," she signaled from the rear deck.

"Good, watch our ass long enough for me to get us out of here."

Riley turned the ship sideways, and circled back towards the fighters. He managed to get two of the seven to shoot at each other as he flew between them, but the other five knew better. Well, that was two fewer. Make that three, Riley smiled as he saw one ship's blip disappear from the monitor, Lara must have gotten him with the cannon.

"You got two coming in at eleven o'clock," she said through the headset.

"I see them, you keep them off my tail and I'll get us out of here alive." Riley really hoped he wasn't lying. He knew the type of ship a Traminian squadron flew, and Bonny was ten times better, but was she better than four of them? He was about to find out.

They were coming at him in a standard V pattern, two from each side with him at the point. As they got closer, they would fire and veer off, Riley knew the drill well. Well enough to counter it with something they'd never seen in their flight schoolbooks. He was counting on that at least.

"They're staying out of range of the guns, and I'm down to my last two cannons." Lara's voice was calm in his ears. His hands began to sweat on the controls. "Come on Bonny, don't let me down."

"They're coming closer, I'm in range with the guns, but they aren't doing much good." Lara's voice was getting a little edgy now, and he could hear her grunt as she worked the guns.

"Their ships are equipped with a force field. Unless you hit the right spot by accident the guns aren't going to do more than annoy them. Just hang tight. I know what I'm doing."

"I hope so. They just got a lock on the ship."

"Good."

Riley slammed the drive up to vertical and flipped Bonny over backwards, shooting at the enemy's fuel tanks as he went. One ship went up in flames, taking its partner out in the ensuing destruction. The other two ships were rocked from the force of the explosion but were still moving.

Pulling out of the flip Riley took advantage of his distance. His ship was made for speed and agility, if he couldn't out-fly these last two he didn't deserve to own Bonny. Zipping around the damaged ships he tried to get enough distance for warp drive. "Bonny, get me the most remote coordinates you have for warp speed!" He could see one of the two survivors, but not the other. Where was the little bastard?

"You see anything yet?"

"Nothing, all clear back here."

"I don't like it. Prepare for warp drive, this could be a bumpy trip."

Bonny's engine whined as she revved up the necessary power. Where were those two? Come on, come on just a little longer and they'd be in the clear.

"Six o'clock! Six o'clock!" Lara warned.

"How many?"

"One."

Riley aimed straight for him. If he wanted to play chicken, so be it. Thirty more seconds and Bonny would have them in another part of space.

"I got the other one in my sights. They're trying a squeeze play, how'd that other one get in front of us?"

"Who cares? Get ready, we're hitting drive in fifteen." Riley locked his focus on the ship ahead of him. Lara only had one cannon left, but he still had both of his. They'd find out which ship had the better weaponry soon. Whoever locked on first would live to fight another day.

"Three o'clock! Three o'clock! That wasn't one of the squadron, we got three, repeat three unfriendlies on us now!"

"Ten more seconds! Do they have a lock?"

"No, but I do." Lara let out a cheer and Riley didn't have to look at the screen to know there'd be one less blip on there.

"Five, four, three, two—" As the warp drive kicked in, Riley felt the ship shudder with the force of an attack.

"We've been hit!" Lara shouted, even as the warp drive pounded him into his seat.

No shit. "Bonny, damage report!"

"Damage to cargo bay, heavy fire taken in right rear quadrant, electrical systems on emergency override. Manual control is advised."

The instrumentation was going haywire. Riley grabbed the controls and tried to plot where they were. Stars flew past them in a blur, and the normal roughness of warp drive was mild in comparison to their present state. Bonny tumbled through space like socks in a zero-g dryer.

"What the hell is going on?! I heard the damage report."

"Then you know as much as I do. Stay put while I try to ride this out."

Cold sweat broke out on his forehead and his knees were like water, but his hands remained steady on the controls as he tried to ride out the drive. When they finally spewed out of warp space, Bonny continued to tumble a few more times before he could control her.

They made it! They got away safely! Only, where were they?

Chapter Eight

"Wahoo! Damn that was some ride!" Lara heard Riley shout through the headset.

Yeah, some ride. They were lucky they were even alive and he was crowing about it like it was the newest ride at an adventure planet. She threw the headset down in disgust. This is why she hated civilian life. Nothing ever went according to plan. Stars! They didn't even have a plan.

This whole situation had her pissed off, and more than a little bit scared. Her entire life had been ordered, routine, by the book. She'd grown up in the military, spent her whole life wearing what she was told, going where she was told, and for the most part doing as she was told. This running willy-nilly all over space made her teeth grind.

Lara unstrapped herself from the gunner's chair and headed back towards the cockpit. Or at least she tried to. One of the damn scarves was caught on a loose piece of metal and had her trapped. Screw it. She ripped the stupid piece of material and kept walking.

She needed some clothes. Her uniform would be best, but she'd take anything at this point. Lara needed to reestablish some control over the mission, and she couldn't very well do that standing half-naked in what was left of her costume and a pair of sewage-encrusted boots.

Tumbling her way towards the cabin, she debated taking the disgusting boots off, but decided she was better stinky than with an object impaled in her foot. The closer she got to the cabin, the worse the destruction was. Lights blinked on and off, and sparks arced overhead. This couldn't be good.

And it wasn't.

The section of the ship that contained the cabin and the cargo holds was now in shambles. There was smoking wreckage everywhere, surrounded by the now hardening emergency foam. The cabin must have taken the brunt of the hit. She was lucky she had been in the gunner's chair instead of hiding in the cabin or she would have been dead and gone before the foam could seal up the damage. Stars, even her uniform couldn't survive devastation like that.

A low whistle sounded behind her. She spun around to see Riley casually eyeing the damage.

"*Feck.* Good thing we weren't in there or we'd be space toast."

"Is that all you have to say?"

"What do you want me to say? We're alive aren't we? Seems to me that's a cause for celebration, not crying because I might have lost a few trinkets."

"I don't see anything to celebrate. We're lost in some forsaken corner of space, the ship is damaged beyond repair, our clothes have been destroyed, and so have the cleaning facilities! What the hell, let's party! Whoopee!" Lara kicked her shit-covered boot at the nearest wall.

"Would you just calm down?"

"I am calm, believe me, this is calm. You don't want to see me when I get upset."

"Relax then. First of all, the ship is not damaged beyond repair, just the landing gear and the electrical systems. I can fix those, it is just going to take some time and some creativity. Second, we can still wash up, it just won't be in a unit; we'll do it the old-fashioned way with water and soap. I keep some on hand for emergencies. As for the clothes, we'll see what I have in the cargo hold; in the meantime you can wear this." Riley unbuttoned his shirt and handed it to her.

"The cargo hold got hit too." Lara took the shirt, doing her best to avoid touching his hand.

"The main cargo hold did, but I have others."

"What do you mean? I haven't seen any." The shirt was soft to the touch, and held the warmth and smell of his body. She laced it up as high as she could, but the tops of her breasts were still on display. At least the darn thing was long, it came almost to her knees. She rolled the sleeves back and glared at Riley, daring him to say something.

He cleared his throat and took his eyes off her breasts. "You aren't supposed to. This ship was owned by an independent contractor—"

"A smuggler, let's just call a spade a spade here." She had to do a little throat clearing herself. His shirt had hidden a washboard stomach and delicious pecs. His little brown male nipples were standing out from a thatch of hair, just begging for her mouth. The familiar feeling of fire in her veins started to flow through her again, making her knees tremble, and her core dampen. Dampen? More like drench. Her pussy was getting so swollen it was like she had a foreign object between her legs. She'd like to get *his* foreign object between her legs.

"Smuggler, independent businessman, whatever. Bonny has some tricks you've never seen. I'll help you wash up and then we can see what we can find."

"I can wash myself, thanks. I've had survival training. I think I remember how it works."

"Sure you don't need someone to wash your back?" Riley asked with such a hot look she was surprised the shirt didn't go up in flames. His eyes roved over her body with an almost palpable thoroughness. He hadn't moved a muscle from his stance across the hall, but she could feel his gaze stripping her naked.

Part of her really didn't mind it either.

Shaking herself out of the sensual daze she had fallen into, Lara shot him another glare. "The soap and water?"

"Right this way, Sweet Cheeks."

She ground her teeth at his nickname, but held her tongue. She really wanted to get clean. Even if she had to use something as barbaric as soap, it would still be better than feeling sweaty and dirty. Riley handed her the soap and showed her how to get hot water from the kitchen unit. Every time he accidentally brushed against her, Lara felt her pulse race and her breathing quicken. She wished he'd get away from her.

Yeah, right. Then why was she so overheated she could practically steam the water all on her own?

"I'll be looking around for something for you to wear while you clean up. When you're done I'll take my turn."

"Fine. Thanks"

Lara turned her back and waited until she heard him leave before she stripped off the shirt and ruined scarves. She put the boots in the cleaning unit. It would either clean them or recycle them as garbage, either way she was rid of them. The scarves she left in a heap on the floor. Good riddance.

It took her a few tries to get the right amount of lather to wash up, but eventually she felt like the dirt was finally off. Doing her hair with a little cup of water and soap was a nightmare, she was going to have to comb it and let it dry by itself before she rebraided it. Normally the unit washed it and combed it for her. Maybe she should cut it short in case this ever happened again.

Wait a minute! Ever happened again? This was never going to happen again. She was going to get control of this situation and get it solved, then she could go back to her normal, everyday life just the way she liked it.

"Here, try these." Riley's hand reached around the doorway, holding a black dress and a pair of boots.

Lara pulled them out of his hand without a word. She just wanted to be decently dressed again. It seemed like she had been naked, or nearly naked, around him ever since she met him.

This wasn't much better.

The dress was as skintight as her uniform, but only came to about three inches below her butt. The top covered more than Riley's shirt, but was so tight it pushed her breasts up higher than ever. The boots were good at least. They came up to above her knee, almost mid-thigh. If the skirt was a little longer, or she was a little shorter she might not feel like a pleasure planet entertainer.

"Uh, do you have anything else?" she asked without coming out of the room.

"Nope, the only other thing I have is even smaller than that. I have plenty of scarves left if you want to stay dressed like a concubine."

"No thanks. Bunny is dead and gone for good."

"Bunny is just a name for any concubine, there are plenty more of them out there," he laughed.

"I was wondering about that." Lara opened the door and handed Riley his shirt. She had been tempted to wear it over the latest getup, but being surrounded by his musky, male scent was doing strange things to her concentration. "Thanks for the shirt. It's your turn."

Lara fled from the look in his eyes and hid out in the cockpit before she could give into temptation and ask if he wanted his back washed.

* * * * *

Riley stood in the hall watching Lara strut by. Her hair practically went down to her ass! And what an ass it was too. Those strides of hers made the dress hike up enough for him to get a great view of her cheeks and a peek at the flesh between her legs. He felt his cock harden yet again at the thought of pumping into her from behind, this time with all that hair spilling over her naked body.

Damn, getting pseudo-leather pants off over a hard-on was not going to be easy. Too bad that was all he had left, well these and a pair of loose pants that looked like they could double as pajamas for Abu the Tentmaker.

Riley got more water for his own bathing, and picked up the soap from where Lara had neatly stored it. He washed his upper body first, trying to give his lower extremities a chance to calm down a little before he pulled the pants off. If he didn't get some relief soon, the pajamas were going to start looking pretty good.

Reaching for something to dry his face off with, he grabbed the first cloth that met his hand, one of Lara's scarves. Wiping his face off, he could smell her woman's scent. His dick jumped right back up at the images the smell of the scarf presented. He could picture in his mind the way her ass thrust up in the air when she was searching the room, the way her breasts jiggled when she was bouncing on the bed, and blast it all, he could remember how they tasted in his mouth and he wanted more.

Much more.

Man, he couldn't figure her out. She was all military this and regulation that, but when he touched her she caught fire. And that dance! He was surprised the entire place didn't catch fire from the way she strutted around the room, rolling her hips and shaking her ass.

Okay, these thoughts were not helping the situation any. He needed to get Bonny repaired, and he couldn't do that until he got his act together. Hell, he didn't even know where they were anyway.

Riley tried to peel the pseudo-leather pants off his hips, but his erection made unfastening the zipper much too risky. He thought about his old Drill Sergeant, but even that wasn't enough to calm his raging hard-on. The cup of cold water sat next to him. His balls tightened up at the idea, but his shaft remained hard as steel.

He could wait until nature took care of things, but as horny as he was right now it could take days for his cock to come down. There was no help for it. If he wanted to get these damn pants off and get clean, he had to take drastic measures. Riley grabbed the water and splashed it on his groin before he could change his mind.

The freezing cold water made his dick shrink painfully fast. He used more cold water to wash up and rinse too. If he had to be around Lara much longer, he was going to need to dunk himself under the waterspout on a regular basis. He slipped his shirt back on, and immediately smelled Lara again. This had to stop. Scooping up the tattered remains of her costume, Riley dumped them in the cleaning unit, impulsively holding back one scarf and sticking it in his shirt.

As he headed back to the cockpit, he watched Lara furiously working the computer on the console. Hold on here a minute! He didn't care how hot she got him, no one messed with Bonny.

"What the *feck* do you think you're doing?"

"I'm trying to find our coordinates, but the electrical system is fried."

"No kidding. I'll take care of it. Keep your hands off my ship."

"Oh, you'll take care of it will you? Just like you took care of everything so far? We've run from one mess to another and have taken more damage with every move. No more! It's time this was run like a military operation, and since I'm the highest- ranking officer here, I'll take command." Her arms crossed over her chest and her eyes shot daggers at him.

Like *fecking* hell she'd take command! This was his ship and she could spout orders all she wanted, didn't mean he was going to listen. She might be the highest-ranking officer, but not in *his* army. It was about time Major Spacer-Babe learned a lesson.

"Listen, Sweet Cheeks, I don't give a damn who you are or what you were. You're ass-deep in trouble right now, and I'm the only one who can help you." Let's see how she liked that little gamma bomb.

"What's that supposed to mean?"

"It means, you could start by listening to me and letting me think of a way out of here."

"You? I'm supposed to listen to you, a randy Traminian smuggler who thinks with his dick instead of the brain you were born with? And what am I supposed to do?"

"You could try being grateful for a change."

"Oh, I should throw myself at you in gratitude because you found me in space, by accident? I don't think so." Lara uncrossed her arms and started to walk past him. *Toradal-shit*. She wasn't going to throw an opening like that at him then walk away.

He grabbed her arm as she tried to brush by. "No, you'll throw yourself at me because you are just as hot for me as I am for you."

Her lip curled up in a sneer. "If your ego gets any bigger we'll have to get you a new helmet. Even if you were the last man alive—"

"I wouldn't finish that sentence if I were you."

She raised one eyebrow at him in challenge. "Oh yeah? Why not?"

"You don't look like the type who likes to be proven wrong." *Come on, take the bait and put me out of my misery.*

"You are so full of yourself." She tried to pull her arm away.

"I'm so right and you know it."

"Oh, please." This time a snort accompanied the lip curl.

She might be acting disgruntled, but her eyes were dilated with desire, and he could feel the heat of her arousal coming off her body.

"Baby, you've been asking for this all day." Riley used his grip on her arm to propel her against the wall before she had a chance to react. Using his lower body, he pinned her and plundered her mouth.

She struggled weakly at first to move her head, but he cupped her face in his hand and held it steady. Lara gave a weak moan, then wrapped her free arm around his neck and pulled him closer.

Yes!

Hoping he didn't have to worry about bodily harm any longer, Riley released her other arm and let his hands roam freely. She wasn't like any other woman he'd ever touched before. Her shoulders were muscular, her body strong, but oh-so-soft in all the right places.

Grazing the tops of her breasts just made him hungry for more. Riley remembered the feel of her from before and was desperate to touch all of her again. Slipping the straps of the dress down, her bounty spread out before him. He released her lips almost reluctantly, but just had to feel her nipples again.

This time, he devoted his attention to one creamy globe at a time. Riley loved how Lara's nipples were so big and responsive to his touch. He sucked at them so hard it was pressed to the roof of his mouth. Her sighs were music to his ears. When she wrapped one of her gorgeous legs around him and pressed her hot, wet cleft against his thigh, he thought he'd died and gone to heaven.

Riley moved to the other nipple and slid his hand across her stomach, pushing her dress down until he could brush against the sweet flesh calling to him. Her breath gasped out in little pants across his cheek as his finger slipped into her hot pussy. Lara's muscles squeezed his finger like a fist and he almost came in his pants at the thought of what they could do to his dick.

His blood was pounding in his ears, and his breathing was none too steady either. He wanted to explore every inch of her luscious body, with his hands, his lips, his tongue. Moving to her neck, he sucked at the vein pulsing so rapidly under her creamy skin. When he slid a second finger inside her sheath, the blood moved even more rapidly.

Lara's hands explored the skin under his shirt. Her fingers pinched his nipples and trailed through the hair on his chest, making even more blood rush to his erection. Lust was shooting fast and hard through his body, pounding through his veins. Sharp nails dug into his muscles, making him growl in response. His control hung on by the thinnest of threads, and it took every last ounce of his willpower to give her one last chance to back out before it was too late.

"I have never wanted anyone like I want you. If this isn't what you want, you better tell me now because I can't take much more," he warned her.

She never got a chance to reply. Wires began sparking around them, lights burnt out with mini explosions, and the automatic warning system began blaring deafening alarms overhead.

Riley watched as she visibly became Major McDaniel again. The hot, wanton woman who was egging him on disappeared beneath the military personae.

"This isn't over, Lara." The storm of desire in his body was still raging, even as she moved away from him.

"Oh, I think it is." She turned her back on him and repaired her appearance before leaving him to contend with the electrical nightmare in front of him.

Chapter Nine

Lara knew she was running away, and for once in her life didn't much care. Her legs could barely support her, and she could still feel the pressure of Riley's mouth on her breasts, the friction of his fingers inside her.

And stars, how she wanted more. That alone was enough to scare her half to death. When you wanted something this badly, it only led to disappointment when you didn't get it.

But what if you did get it?

That would probably lead to even more disappointment. In her experience, the foreplay was always much better than the actual sex. Forget having a climax, her sex life was the anticlimax. Once the sex started, any hope of coming ended.

But that wasn't what she was afraid of now, was it? The little annoying voice in the back of her head dug the knife in a little harder. She wasn't afraid that the sex wouldn't be as good as the buildup, she was afraid it would be better. Pacing, Lara tried to think her way through this mess her hormones were creating in her normally rational brain.

She could have sex with Riley; it wasn't like she was a virgin or anything. She'd never really formed any attachments with any of her sexual partners before, what was different about this?

For starters, she was always the one who set the ground rules and the boundaries before. Lara was positive Riley would break through any boundaries she set. As exciting as that was, it didn't leave her any room to escape from him unscathed. In the past, her position had kept her moving around the galaxy so she didn't have to worry about breaking things off; her job did it for her. Since she didn't sleep with anyone in her troop, she didn't have to worry about dealing with ongoing relationships either.

Even if she could walk away from Riley, where could she go? Stars, she didn't even know where she was right now. Well, she wasn't going to find out hiding in the kitchen like some Nervous Nelly on prom night. Suck it up and get over it. If she just put the mission ahead of everything else she would be fine.

Right. The annoying voice mocked her.

Squaring her shoulders, she took a deep, somewhat shaky breath and marched back to the cockpit. She needed to see what she could do to help get them out of here and find her Emperor. Remember him? The reason she was doing all of this?

Her self-scolding didn't seem to help focus her thoughts much when she spotted Riley flat on his back with his shirt off. He was laying down under the console muttering to himself. One leg was bent at the knee giving her a tantalizing view of his attributes. Every once in a while he'd reach out and grab a tool and mutter some more. Each time he moved, the muscles of his stomach rippled and rolled in a mesmerizing display.

Lara stood there dumbfounded just watching his torso move. Her already sensitized nerves reminded her that she could have him if she wanted.

She could crawl right on top of him and lick her way from his belly button to his neck. She could suck his nipples in her mouth like he did to her, reach into those tight pants and stroke the package that was so deftly outlined by the pseudo-leather.

Her knees grew weak at the prurient thoughts spinning in her brain. What would the harm be? Just a quick fuck, relieve the need and get it out of the way. It was interfering with the mission anyway. Yeah, she'd do this for her Emperor.

Who the stars was she kidding? Fuck Riley for the Emperor? She would not lie to herself or justify the situation. *Pull yourself together, McDaniel!*

"Can you figure out the malfunction?" Her voice was throatier than normal. She hoped he wouldn't notice.

"What? Ouch! Damn!" Riley banged his head as he slid out from under the console to look at her.

"I asked if you knew what the problem was." Lara focused her gaze on a light two inches to the left of his head. It was the only way she could think straight.

"Yeah, I know what it is. The blast fried one of the nerve centers in the electrical system. I can fix it, but it will take a few days. I have to replace all the circuits along the nerve that got hit. And by the way, I also figured out where we are." He had a cocky grin on his face, like he knew why she wouldn't meet his gaze.

"And where is that?" Focus on the mission, focus on the mission.

"We are orbiting the second moon of the planet Syder, and that is a bit of luck, if I do say so myself."

"Oh really? How do you figure that? Syder is clear across the galaxy from Emeraldia and Tramin."

"Exactly." His smug smile was taking the edge off her raging hormones.

"Stop playing games and spit it out, Flyboy. I'm in no mood for Twenty Questions."

"You take all the fun out of things."

"Exactly," she mocked him. "This isn't supposed to be fun; this is a job not a game. My job, now spit it out so I can make a plan." *And get my mind off your hot bod.*

"You and your *fecking* plans." He heaved a heavy sigh. "From what Dolf told me, a Traminian squadron flew to a deserted mining asteroid in this corner of space a few days ago."

"So?"

"So, there is no reason for a squadron to fly anywhere near here, except if they wanted to dump something they didn't want anyone to see."

"Can you trust this Dolf?" This was as good a lead as anything else they had to go on right now.

"As much as I trust anyone, yeah. He knows if he lies to me and I find out I'll take it out of his hide."

"So where is this mining asteroid?"

"On the outskirts of Syder's other moon."

Lara couldn't believe their luck had actually changed for the better. With the way things were going for the last week, there had to be a trick in here somewhere. "What's the catch?"

"Can't you just enjoy good news?"

"No, there is always a catch. Just when you think you're coming in for a clear landing, someone is there to stick it to you."

"That's a great attitude you have there, Sweet Cheeks. But in this case, you're right. Bonny is going to need some extensive repairs, more than what I can do in orbit, and we are going to have to hire some help if we want to spring your Emperor from his prison. Plus we're going to have to get some more information to find out what we're up against."

"I am not dressing up in that ridiculous costume again!" No sparking way could she go through that again in her present state of sexual awareness.

"Don't worry, you're fine just like that. It's going to take me a few days to get Bonny fixed up enough so we can land on Syder's moon and get some repairs. Then we'll see about how to get your Emperor."

"Fine, the sooner we get him, the sooner I can get back to my life. My normal life."

"What's so bad about what you've been doing lately? It certainly isn't dull."

Lara felt her temper burn through her veins. "Dull? I could handle dull right about now. In fact, dull is looking pretty sparking good to me."

She spun away from him, trying to control her temper. It didn't work. Turning back to face him, she put her hands on her hips and lit into him. "You know something? In the real world, my world, life isn't all about getting laid and having fun. There are responsibilities to be taken care of. I didn't get where I am today by running off to find the next adventure. I worked damn hard and I'm not going to let anyone take it away from me."

"No one is trying to take anything away from you. I'm just saying it's okay to have a little fun now and then. I'll bet you don't even know how to have fun."

"That's not true. I enjoy my job, my life." Well, most of the time anyway.

"Right. When was the last time you took a vacation and went to one of those pleasure planets? Never, I bet." He raised an eyebrow in challenge.

"I don't see how getting drunk and losing all my money would be considered fun."

"Honey, there is a lot more to do there than just drink and gamble."

"Oh yeah, I forgot, you can have sex too. Big deal." It would be a big deal if she were having it with Riley.

"You don't know what you are missing, Sweet Cheeks. I'll tell you what. When I get my reward money from rescuing your Emperor, I'll take you to one of the planets and show you how to have a *fecking* good time."

"No thanks. If we manage, *when* we manage to get the Emperor back, I'm going to be way too busy going after the ones who did this to go gallivanting off for some cheap thrills."

"Your loss, baby." He slid back under the console and began tinkering away again. As he worked, he bent his knee again, which pulled the pants even tighter, outlining his cock perfectly.

Lara remembered the feel of his erection pressed against her naked cleft and felt the burning start all over again. Was he right? Did she not know how to have fun? When all this was over, would she regret not taking the time to find out what she'd been missing?

"Hey, if you're not doing anything, can you check the panel to my left?"

"Sure, anything to get us moving. What am I checking it for?" she asked, moving over to stand next to his sprawled body.

"Tell me if the lights are on, off, or blinking."

"Blinking."

"Damn, okay. Reach over and open the panel. I want you to see if any of the wires in there are loose."

Lara had to step over him, straddling his chest to reach the panel. "Yeah, there are a couple loose, hold on and I'll reconnect them."

"Wait! Not yet!" Riley shouted, just as the fuse blew.

Lara jumped away from the sparking panel, shaking her hand where the wires had burned her fingers.

"Don't touch anything unless I tell you to!" Riley jumped up and pushed by her. He fussed over the fuse box like a protective mother hen with her only chick.

Lara grabbed Riley's arm and spun him around to face her. "I'm not a child and I don't take orders from some scruffy Flyboy!"

"You will when you're on my ship!" he screamed into her face.

Lara wasn't backing down from anyone. She went nose to nose with him. "Oh, yeah? Make me."

The rational part of Lara's brain screamed at her that she had just said what Riley wanted her to. The part that was flooded with hormones was cheering her on.

He didn't bother to answer, just grabbed her head in his hands and pulled it to his in a mind-blowing kiss. She had thought their earlier adventures would have prepared her for this, but nothing could stop the flood of feelings from overwhelming her. Lara didn't want to react, didn't want to become a raging lunatic who let her body control her mind, but she couldn't stop herself from spearing her fingers in his soft sandy hair and dragging him closer.

"There's no escape this time, baby." He pulled his mouth away from hers and looked her in the eyes, his green ones on fire. "I don't care if the Emperor himself and the entire Traminian and Emeraldian armies march through the door. This doesn't stop until I make you mine."

Lara's body was humming with urgency. It had been denied too many times for her to back away now. His words shot a laser bolt of lust straight to her pussy. The rational part of her mind was swamped with lust and the rest of her was rejoicing in the sensations running wild through her system.

"Then what's taking you so long?"

"Not a damn thing." Riley scooped her up and laid her on the pilot's chair. As he sprawled on top of her, she felt the chair shift to accommodate the two of them.

That wasn't all she was feeling either. Riley's teeth were nipping at her lip, drawing it inside his mouth in a sensual buffet. His hands were everywhere, stroking her, teasing her. Making her want more, feel more than she ever had before. Not wasting any more time, Riley pulled the dress off her body and flung it to the floor. As she leaned down to undo the boots, he stopped her.

"No, leave them on, I've wanted to see you in nothing but those boots since the second you put them on."

"Fine with me, saves time," Lara gasped as he pulled her nipple into his mouth, his hand kneading the other one.

He may want her to leave the boots on, but she wanted to see him completely naked. She struggled with the tight, pseudo-leather pants trying to tug them over his hips.

"Slow down, slow down. I'll do it." Riley stood up and carefully stripped the tight pseudo-leather down his body.

And what a body it was. The slim waist she had been ogling since he took his shirt off trailed down to washboard abs and ropey, muscular thighs. It was what was between those thighs that took her breath away though. Springing from a thatch of curly hair was his shaft, standing up proud and strong. Lara had never seen such a well-endowed male before, and it made her a little nervous. And very excited.

The urge to touch him was overwhelming. Giving into the need driving her, Lara got off the chair and went to her knees in front of him. She grasped his shaft in one hand and stroked its velvety length. His penis was rock-hard and jumped as she stroked it. He was so hot and ready for her, she just had to lean in and taste the fluid that pearled at the swollen tip. One taste wasn't nearly enough. Releasing the length of him, she grabbed onto his muscled butt and pulled him deeper into her mouth. His breath exploded out over her and she hummed in smug satisfaction.

"Blast, that feels good. Too good." He thrust deeper, and Lara could feel him at the back of her throat, she sucked him as hard as she could, wanting to make him as crazy for her as she was for him.

"This is not going to last very long if you keep that up," Riley said, slowly pulling away and lifting her back onto the chair.

"What's wrong? Can't handle the pressure?" she taunted.

"Let's see how well you react under pressure, Sweet Cheeks."

Riley flipped her over onto her stomach and straddled her hips. His lightly-furred legs made delicious friction everywhere they touched. When he slid lower, the sensation set her nerves on fire. What had she gotten herself into?

"Man, have I wanted to get my hands on this ass of yours. Relax, Baby, this is going to take a while."

Lara felt Riley's calloused fingers skimming the cheeks of her butt. The contrast of his slightly rough fingers sliding over the smooth globes of her cheeks sent flames of heat straight to her center. Her body was so sensitive to his every touch, at this point he could touch her fingernails and it would feel erotic. The sensations were exquisite, but it wasn't going to break her. She could wait him out in this game.

Her legs were still pressed tightly together, and she felt her pussy lips pulse and swell. They were slippery with her fluid, and she was sure the chair would be drenched by the time she got up again. Riley slid a little further down her legs, still running his fingers lightly over her skin, barely touching it. She was getting more antsy now, when would he get to the good parts?

"How you doin' there, sweetheart?"

"Just fine, how 'bout you?" Her breathing was coming a little heavier now, but she was still okay. If he would just hurry!

"Oh, I'm doing great. I've got the best view in the house. Do you know you have a little dimple right here?"

Riley kissed the spot she obviously couldn't see at the base of her spine. His hot breath spread out over her, and when he started giving nipping kisses down her cheeks to the curve where her ass met her legs, she thought she was going to explode.

Every nerve she possessed seemed to jump out of her skin. Her thighs were slippery with the cream that was flowing from her pussy and her clit begged to be touched. Lara felt his mouth near her weeping cleft and almost moaned in supplication. Almost. Biting her lip, she managed to keep silent, but nothing could stop her from lifting her hips up and spreading her legs as wide as her position allowed her.

"Something I can help you with, sweetheart?" Riley murmured into her thigh. He moved so that he was kneeling between her spread legs, pushing them open even farther.

Lara had lost the power of speech; all she could do was whimper as his fingers trailed along the outskirts of her folds. His touch was feather-light and frustrating as hell.

"You are so hot and wet for me. Do you know how it makes me feel to know that all of this is for me?" Riley asked as he dipped his finger further into her well and rubbed his fingers against her slick walls.

Lara was going to chew a hole through her lip if he didn't do something soon. The feeling of his finger pumping in and out of her, but not rubbing her clit was making her lose her mind. He pulled her up so she was on her hands and knees in front of him. The position left her weeping core wide open for him, and stars, she wished he'd fill her.

When she felt the tip of his penis rubbing in the cream that was preparing her for his entry she almost wept in relief.

"What do you want, Lara? Tell me."

"I want you in me. Now!"

"I should have known you would be bossy about this, too."

Riley didn't shove himself in like she wanted him to, instead he slipped the rounded tip barely inside her grasping body.

"More! I want all of you in me."

"And you'll have me sheathed to the hilt, but we'll do it my way."

"Bastard," Lara said weakly. She was sweating, actually sweating from wanting him so badly. Her breathing was coming out in gasps, and her legs trembled from the pressure she was putting on them not to move.

"You sweet talker you. Now be a good girl and I'll give you more."

"If you give me more, I'll show you just how good I can be," Lara challenged him.

Riley didn't seem to need any more encouragement, but slammed himself inside her with enough force to send her flying over the edge before he had even stopped moving. She let out a high, sharp scream as her body exploded into a million, throbbing pieces.

* * * * *

The feeling of Lara's muscles milking him made Riley clench his teeth and pray for mercy. There was no way he was going to last much longer. It had been torture enough stopping before he was fully inside her. All he wanted to do now was slam repeatedly against her precious ass until he was drained.

"Lara, I'm not going to last much longer if you keep squeezing me like that."

"No problem, do whatever makes you happy. I'm just going to lay here for a while until my body reforms." The dreamy tone of voice was all the permission he needed.

Spreading her hair out over her back, Riley grabbed her ass and pumped his hips into her at a warp speed of his own. He had been fighting the feeling for so long, when his come jetted its way through his body he could have sworn his heart stopped. He thrust a few more times after spending his load, but the sensation was almost too good to bear. Riley knew he'd never had better sex in his life, but damn if he'd admit it.

"Not bad for an appetizer," he murmured, pulling out of her and rolling to the side of the chair. Good thing it was adjustable or they would have ended up on the floor.

"If that was the appetizer, I can't wait to see the main meal."

"We've got an all-you-can-eat buffet here, sweetie. Eat your fill." He sprawled out so she could get a good look at him. He was so relaxed now she could have asked to paint him blue and he wouldn't have cared.

Lara didn't say anything, just got up and moved around the chair until she was in front of him. His dick perked up at the sight of her standing there in nothing but thigh-high boots. Her breasts were lush and a little red from where his stubble had rubbed against the tender flesh. Riley watched as she lifted one foot up on the chair and unzipped a boot. He got a great view of her cleft and had to swallow as his mouth watered. He had been in too much of a rush last time. This time he would savor every delicious taste and scent of her.

The other boot soon followed the first, and Lara stood in front of him wearing nothing but yards of hair. "I think I'm getting hungry, but the feast doesn't look quite prepared yet," she said, indicating his semi-flaccid penis.

"Give me a few minutes, darlin' and you'll have more than you can handle." He'd show her what he could do, once he had sufficiently recovered.

"Guess I'll just have to start without you then." She looked him right in the eye and started to fondle her own breasts. Lifting one scrumptious globe in her hand, she pinched the nipple and bent her head to suck it into her mouth.

His recovery time was going to break new records if she kept this up. Releasing the nipple from her mouth, Lara continued to pinch and play with her own nipples while she used her other hand to run down her stomach into the curly hair that hid her folds. She lifted one foot back onto the chair so he got a front row view of her fingers going in and out of her body. Her thumb circled her nub while her fingers drove in and out of her slippery pussy.

Riley was fully ready and functioning now, but he was so enthralled watching her pleasure herself he kept silent. Her head was thrown back, and her hair brushed the upper swells of her butt. Her nipples were red from her ministrations of them, and he could see the come streaming out of her body as she used her hips to thrust onto her hand. When she bucked and groaned, Riley had to dig his hands into his thighs to keep from coming with her. His head swam with lust and amazement. He was inches away from his own climax, and she hadn't even touched him. Blast! He'd only just come out of her after having the most amazing orgasm of his life, and already he was seconds from another one.

"Umm, that was yummy. Sorry I didn't wait for you." She didn't seem in the least bit sorry in his opinion, but he didn't really care.

"I'm ready for a little snack myself. Why don't you lay down and relax?" She wouldn't be relaxed for long. He was going to make sure of it.

He got up as she sauntered over, her sex kitten act ruined by the obvious shaking of her knees. She might be trying to fool him into believing she did this all the time, but he knew better. This was a new experience for her, and he was going to make sure she never had another one like it.

"Make yourself comfortable," he said, handing her a pillow from the bench under the chair.

"If I get any more comfortable I'll slip into a coma." She laced her fingers behind her head and closed her eyes anyway.

"Don't mind me, I'm just going to nibble a little bit first." Riley pulled her foot up and massaged the arch while he sucked on her toe. Applying just the right amount of pressure, he waited for her reaction. When her eyes flew open and her hips came off the chair bucking rapidly, he knew he'd found the right spot.

Continuing to suck and nibble along the curve of her foot, he made his way past her ankle, up her calf to the sensitive spot behind her knee. He still had her foot raised in one hand, and he used his free one to wander over her body in feather-light caresses.

When he got to her inner thigh, Riley dropped her foot and went to work on her other one, treating it to the same sensuous torture. As his hands crept up her thighs close to the soaking wet center of her, he could hear her breath coming in gasps. She had told him that she'd never had a screaming orgasm before. He aimed to change that.

Her long, beautiful legs were all his to explore. He wanted to spend hours touching every inch of them. "You have the best legs I've ever seen, do you know that?" He massaged her thighs, digging his fingers into the muscle of them, then soothing with the pads of his fingers. "I thought your ass was the best thing I'd ever come across, but I'm not so sure anymore. These muscles make you so sensitive to my every touch. It is terribly arousing." Did her legs taste as sweet as the rest of her? He moved his head to her thigh and licked his way up.

"Tell me about it!" she gasped out at him.

Riley laughed to himself against the juncture of her thighs. She was so responsive to his every touch. Desire slammed into his gut as he felt a quiver go through her body. She was so close to coming, but he wasn't going to let her fly yet. He wanted to make this the best *fecking* orgasm she ever had, and he'd do that by holding her off as long as possible.

"Oh no, not yet. I'm not nearly ready to put down my plate." He wanted her orgasm to fry her brain, and he didn't think the heat was hot enough yet. Backing away from the temptation of her cleft, he licked his way up the hollow of her hips and pelvis. Twirling his tongue in her belly button, he inched his fingers up until he could squeeze her breasts again. His chest was against her center, and he could feel her wetness on his naked body. She might not be the only one having a screaming orgasm.

Riley ran his fingers between the lower slopes of her breasts and the top of her mons. Here was his own path to ecstasy. Her eyes were completely dilated and her head thrashing. She was riding the crest of the wave yet again. Watching her build was almost as exciting as watching her come, but it wasn't time yet.

Taking his hands completely, if reluctantly, off her body Riley positioned himself over her. His cock was poised at her entrance and his chest just barely touching hers. He leaned his head down to take her mouth in a kiss that was meant to destroy any remaining composure. Instead, it was she who scorched him by grabbing his hips and pushing his shaft into her sheath.

"Oh my stars!" she groaned.

Groaning was good, but he wanted a screaming orgasm. Riley slid his hands under her ass and lifted her higher. Positioning himself on his knees, he began to slowly glide in and out of her. He moved and adjusted until he could find her hot spot. When her hips pistoned up and began thrusting around him he knew he had found the right one.

Her screams echoed through the ship only seconds before his own shout rang out.

Chapter Ten

The sounds of metal clanging against metal woke Lara up. She had drifted as soon as Riley pulled out of her. Drifted off or passed out from an overdose of pleasure. Either way she felt rested and refreshed.

The cockpit reeked of the musk of sweat and sex. Lara felt sore in muscles she didn't even know she had, and she was sticky with the results of their all-night orgy. All in all, she was messy, sore, and damn satisfied.

Riley tinkered under Bonny's console with his shirt off. Rolling onto her side she watched the play of muscles in Riley's abdomen as he reached for tools and fiddled with whatever mysterious components were absorbing his attention. If it wasn't for the desperate need to pee, Lara could have watched him all day. Too bad she really had to use the facilities.

Grabbing his shirt off the floor, Lara slipped it over her head. In bare feet, she padded to the mini unit they were using for a refreshing unit until they could get the repairs done. She wiped the fluids between her legs off the best she could with soap and water. It did the job, but she would feel better when she could get really clean again. Not that the lack of facilities would stop her from having another go with Riley. Mind-blowing sex was worth a bit of discomfort afterwards.

Lara grabbed a cup of syntho-coffee and sat down on the bench. Man, who would have thought a basic bodily function like sex could make you feel so different? She'd had sex before, but the difference between her previous experiences and the galactic cruise she and Riley had completed was night and day. Riley had kissed, licked, and caressed every inch of her. If he missed a spot or two it wasn't for lack of trying.

She'd never felt so beautiful, so *cherished* in her entire life. Being raised in a military orphanage wasn't exactly a touchy-feely upbringing. As a general rule Lara wasn't a demonstrative person, but Riley had blown through any barriers she could erect before she could even think about building them. Maybe her past lovers weren't strong enough to push past the walls she'd built? Who knew it could be so much fun letting go of all that control?

Snorting, Lara pushed herself to her feet. She hadn't let go of any control. Riley had taken it from her without a hint of protest on her part. That was a good thing for sex, but was that a good thing for when they were out of bed? Did he think just because they had good sex he could take over now? No way! She'd see how he behaved before she overreacted, but just because he'd given her mind numbing orgasms didn't mean she was going to bow down to his wishes.

Squaring her shoulders, Lara rinsed out her cup and marched back to the cockpit. She'd show him she was no pushover.

Riley was whistling and tapping his foot while still puttering under the console. Stars, but the man was good enough to eat. *Stop that! Get your mind out of his pants and focus!* Her eyes strayed to the juncture regardless of what her brain was saying.

"So how long until we can land on the moon, and how long do you think it will take to get this tub repaired once we get there?" Lara forced herself to be all business now.

Riley banged his head on the console before he slid out to look at her. "Could you cough or something so I know you're there? For a big woman you sure do move quietly."

"So sorry to bother you, I was just wondering when we could finish this little vacation here and get back to work. You know what work is, don't you?" She couldn't believe she was hurt by him saying she was a big woman. She was a big woman after all. Maybe he was just used to those midget concubines from Tramin. Well screw him, she wasn't going to apologize for her height and strength. Both had served her better in her life than being petite ever could. She'd like to see one of those mini concubines take out half a Traminian Special Ops squadron.

"I told you it is going to take a few days to get this fixed, then we can land and get the rest of Bonny fixed up. What jet got up your ass?"

"I don't have any jet up my ass, I'm just getting a little anxious to be moving. You know it's my job on the line if I can't get the Emperor back."

"I know, I know. You've told me a thousand times about your precious job. What's the big deal anyway? What's the worst that could happen if you lost your job?"

"That is the worst thing that could happen to me! You have no idea how hard it is for someone with my background to work my way into the upper ranks of the army. Not only am I from the orphanage, I'm a woman. I've had to do everything twice as good, work twice as hard, and put up with twice the amount of crap to get where I am today." Lara couldn't even fathom what would happen if she lost her job. Her entire life was defined by her rank, her position. If she lost that, she'd lose everything.

"There's more to life than your job. Any job."

"Not for me there isn't."

"Then I feel sorry for you." He picked up another tool off the floor. "If I work through the night I could have this fixed by tomorrow." Riley slid back under the console, but he was no longer whistling.

What did he know anyway? Lara picked up her dress that was still lying on the floor. He didn't know what it was like to have to fight for every little thing. A person learned damn fast how to fight to survive when there were thirty kids to a room and only food and beds for twenty-five. She'd like to see him put up with doing all the shit jobs just so he could get noticed and move up a measly rank.

She flopped down on the chair, trying not to remember all the things they had done on it the night before. He said if he worked all night they could land tomorrow. Looked like there would be no repeat of last night's orgasm feast.

Something Riley did must have worked because the vid screen came to life suddenly. Lara was about to turn off the ear-crunching music vid that was on when it was interrupted by a news-flash. Empress Lisandra was standing at a podium preparing to speak. Her hair was curled into golden spirals that bounced around her porcelain features. Her tiny hands seemed to be shaking as she fiddled with the microphone.

Lara had had limited dealings with the Empress, Lisandra preferred her bodyguards to be men. Muscular, good-looking men at that. Lara didn't blame her. Emperor Thomellt was a fat, lecherous old man who chased anything with breasts. It obviously wasn't a love match, and if the Empress wanted to get a little affection on the side, well good for her.

"It is with deep regret that I stand before you today, my Emeraldia family. I can only believe my dear, dear, husband and your Emperor has been killed by the wretched Traminians who kidnapped him from his ship. We still don't know what happened aboard *The Federation*, and the only one who can tell us, we fear is also dead. Let us all remember the bravery of Major Lara McDaniel who died in defense of our beloved Emperor." She paused dramatically to wipe a tear from her eye.

"Even though we mourn for the passing of our dear friends, we must continue with the running of our country." Lara wondered how long the Empress actually mourned. And how many times could she get dear into one speech anyway?

"As my husband would have wished, our son Arto will assume the throne as soon as he reaches majority. In the meantime, I will act as his proxy and assume the role of Commander of the Armies. My first duty shall be to declare war on the Traminians. I must go now and meet with my generals to prepare for this momentous event. Thank you all."

Lara sat back in the chair, stunned. They thought she was dead, and the Empress was declaring war on one of their oldest allies. Had they crossed into a parallel universe somehow?

"Did I just hear that right? Emeraldia is going to war with Tramin?" Riley got up and stood near the vid screen.

"Yup, seems the Empress is assuming the Emperor is dead and is acting as proxy to the heir."

"That happened fast. Wonder what she knows that we don't?"

"What do you mean?" Lara tried to follow his thinking, but the expanse of bare skin he was showing, and its proximity to her mouth was distracting her terribly.

"Well, usually with a kidnapping there is a ransom of some sort. They didn't just kill the Emperor on his ship and blow it up, they kidnapped him. Seems to me the Empress knows he isn't coming back. And why do they think you are dead?"

"I don't know. My homing device—that's it! My homing device is planted in my uniform, which is now just a wisp of space lint. They must have seen it go off and figured I'd been blown to smithereens too."

"That could work in our favor. If they think you're dead they won't be expecting you to mount a rescue attempt."

Lara was about to make a sarcastic comment when Riley held up his hand for silence. She immediately stopped talking and listened. The vid screen had switched to a slightly different news satellite and another talking head was speaking.

"Unnamed sources within the Traminian government compound have leaked information to us that the Emeraldians have declared war on Tramin. We are awaiting word from The Council now."

"This ought to be interesting," Lara muttered, sitting up for a better view.

The vid display crinkled a little until Riley smacked it with his hand, the display cleared. A large walrus of a man waddled out on the steps of the government building.

Behind him was a gray haired man in a military uniform that was covered in medals and ribbons.

"That must be Rody, right?" Lara said, indicating the Military Commander of Tramin.

"Yeah, the bastard."

"Not your best friend I take it."

"He's the reason I'm flying around looking for space junk instead of leading my squad. Yeah, you could say we aren't exactly bosom buddies."

"Citizens of Tramin, disturbing news has been delivered to The Council by military sources. Emeraldia has blamed us for the disappearance of their Emperor, an obviously trumped-up charge, and has formally declared war on Tramin."

"That was fast. Your spies must be better than we gave them credit for," Lara said absently.

"How do you know about spies in the palace?"

"I'm the Emperor's personal bodyguard; I make it my point to know everyone in the palace. I figured better the ones I know than ones I don't, so I never bothered to kick them out. You'd only replace them and I'd have to do new background checks. Easier just to assign watchers to them."

Riley was about to say something else but stopped when Rody stepped forward to speak.

"We will persevere in this time of difficulty. As is written in our charter, during times of war Martial Law will be enacted. As the highest ranking commander, I will assume command until the Emeraldians are ground into dust beneath our heels!"

The crowd cheered as Rody raised his fist in the air. The councilor behind him looked a little sick, but managed to smile weakly as Rody led him off the steps.

"Did he just say what I thought he said?" Lara asked in disbelief. "I thought Tramin was a republic? Aren't your councilors voted into office by the people? How can one man take control of the entire planet?"

"A long time ago someone figured out that you can't win a war by committee, so the powers that be decided that in times of war one leader must take command. Since most of the councilors have very limited military experience, it was decided that the Chief Military Commander would be the one to take control. Once a peace treaty is signed, he steps down and The Council takes over again."

"Makes sense I guess. I mean, most military leaders know more about knocking things down than building them back up, but wars can last years, decades even."

"I know. That's what bothers me so much. Tell me about the Empress." Riley leaned back against the console.

"What's there to tell? She looks like a little doll and acts like one too. She spends her days having her hair and nails done, then goes to tea with her ladies and attends luncheons and balls. She is more of an ornament for the Emperor than anything else. I hope she has kept the Emperor's advisers on because otherwise she is going to run the planet into the ground."

"Okay, so we have your entire crew poisoned by a delivery of meat from the Empress. Traminian Special Ops coming in and kidnapping the Emperor, and I get blamed for his disappearance. Then, we have a full squadron flying after my ship in fighting formation, not trying to stop us for questioning, but trying to kill us. Now you're saying the toy empress is going to play at running the planet and declaring war on Tramin, meanwhile Rody convinces the Council to hand over command because of a two hundred year old loophole in the charter."

"My, my, my, you do have a brain in that head of yours after all."

"Yeah, I have a brain, and I also have a nose, and it smells a conspiracy."

"Give me a break! Lisandra can't even do her hair by herself and you think she was able to organize a coup?"

"No, I think Rody planned and executed it and used your pretty little Empress to help him." Riley tapped his hand against his leg.

"But war isn't good for either planet, it doesn't make any sense." Lara was still trying to figure out how Lisandra could pull off something of this magnitude.

"Sure it does. They don't actually have to go to war; they just have to declare it. Emeraldia can launch a few attacks, Tramin can defend itself, and then they can lie about false battles for years. If anyone gets suspicious, then they can launch another attack. The planets just need to think they are at war, they don't actually have to be in one."

"Okay, I'll give you that, but eventually the heir is going to reach majority. Then what?"

"How old is he now?"

"He's seventeen, he'll assume the throne at twenty-one."

"And what if he has a mysterious accident before then?"

"Come on now! You are saying that Lisandra would kill her husband and her son?"

"It's been known to happen."

"But Lisandra?"

"Okay, try this on for size. If Lisandra is as weak and dingy as you say, how hard would it be for someone to play to her vanity?"

Lara snorted, "Not very."

"So let's say Rody meets her at some function. The Emperor is off chasing a skirt somewhere and Lisandra is all by herself. Rody comes over and tells her how beautiful she is and how badly her husband treats her, blah, blah, blah."

"Right, she is flattered, and they have an affair. Then he convinces her the only way they can be together is if they get rid of her husband—" she trailed off.

"Yeah, and in order to marry her, to be considered worthy of her, he'd have to be equal in status—"

"Which would mean there would have to be a war so he could get control. It makes perfect sense in a twisted, warped sort of way."

"Rody is the king of manipulation. He has all his troops believing every word he says, or he gets rid of them. If he ordered a squad to kidnap the Emperor for the good of the country, they'd do it no questions asked. Idiots." Riley looked disgusted.

"Part of that is just military training. If you argue with every command given to you, you aren't going to win many wars."

"I'll give you that. Soldiers need to listen to their commanders during a battle-type situation, but I'm talking about life. Just because someone is a higher rank than you doesn't mean they are necessarily smarter."

"But they sure think so. I'll bet that was why Rody kicked you out. He knew he couldn't manipulate you."

"Who cares?" Riley shrugged. "That's water under the bridge. Right now we have to get your Emperor back, stop a war, and kick Rody's ass."

"You know, you act so irreverent, the ultimate rebel, but it really is an act, isn't it? You want to do the right thing and get even with Rody for taking away your command."

"I don't know what you are talking about, Sweet Cheeks. I left the military life a long time ago and I don't miss it one bit. I've got my ship, Max, and no one telling me what to do. I like my life just fine the way it is. I'm in this for the money and that's it. Once we get through this I'm going on my merry way."

"Okay." She didn't buy it for a minute.

"I am."

"I know. Don't you think you should get busy so we can land this thing?"

"Don't paint me out to be some vid hero Lara, you'll only be disappointed."

"Don't worry about me Riley, just get this tub fixed so we can get moving, I'm getting a little antsy."

Lara walked out, and almost tripped over the humongous cat, Max. Bending down to scratch him behind the ears, she thought about what Riley had said. He talked a big game, but she knew with every atom of her being there was more to him than the carefree space scavenger he tried to act like. Riley had shown a shipload of ingenuity and skill in their dealings so far; he was wasted floating around aimlessly in space.

Max twined about her feet, rubbing his head into her hand when she stopped scratching. "What do you think, Fat Boy, is Riley really happy cruising around in space instead of leading his troops?"

A loud purring and a "mwerp" was the only answer she got.

* * * * *

Riley watched her go and shook his head. He tried to warn her. It wouldn't be his fault if she got upset when he took off after this was all done. He wasn't the type to stay in any one place for very long, and he certainly wasn't the type to stay with any one woman either.

The last thing he needed was to have some bossy spacer-broad in his life telling him what to do and how to do it. Even if she was the hottest thing in bed he'd ever seen. Hard to believe her uptight military front hid a passionate woman beneath it. Still, sex could only go so far, after that you had to have something in common or they'd be at each other's throats in a month.

No, he was right to warn her off. When this was all over he'd make a clean break and get out of there. Shit, she probably wanted the same thing. She was more interested in her job than in actually having a life.

But when had she ever had a chance at life?

Riley knew about the military orphanages on Emeraldia. Yeah, the government took care of its kids, but that didn't mean they got everything they needed. Kids were broken up into troops by the time they were five years old. They either conformed, or suffered. Every minute of the day was regimented, and planned out for them. When they were old enough to get out, the expectation was they would join the army to pay back the government for supporting them all those years.

No wonder Lara always needed a plan, she'd never been without one.

Hey, that wasn't his problem. Just because they tossed up the sheets didn't mean he had to save her from herself, or she even wanted him to. She seemed bound and determined to go back to her life the way it used to be. Seemed like she was perfectly happy being chased after by her boss, having boring sex, and doing what she was told.

Feck it! It wasn't his job! Thinking about the situation was pissing him off. He needed to concentrate on fixing the electrical and the landing systems. He'd promised Lara he'd work all night on them if he had to. Talk about cutting off your nose to spite your face.

Well, what did he expect? That she was going to fall at his feet and beg him to stop working so they could screw each other's brains out again? Like that was going to happen. Shit, she was using him as much as he was using her. They were in an impossible situation, and the sooner they got out of it the better. He'd do his part.

After he took a little break to see what she was up to.

Where did she go? The ship wasn't that big, and it wasn't like she was so tiny he could miss her. Riley wandered down until he came to what used to be the main room, and was now the only room. Lara had swept all the debris to the side and was doing something that looked almost like a dance, but in slow motion. She was breathing deeply and making motions with hands and body. It was almost like she was in a trance, the way she had her breathing timed to her movements.

Riley watched as she dropped her hands to her sides and bowed. He stayed still as she continued to breathe deeply, he didn't want to break the spell. Finally she opened her eyes and looked at him.

"What's going on?" she asked.

"Nothing, just taking a break. What was that dance thing you were doing?"

"It isn't a dance, it's tai chi, an ancient form of defense and meditation. I was clearing my mind of unnecessary clutter."

"Like me?"

"Maybe. I need to concentrate and having all those hormones running through my system isn't helping any."

Did she really think she could just close her eyes and make it go away? "I don't think it's that easy, Sweet Cheeks."

"Meditation has been used for thousands of years to cleanse one's mind of disturbing emotions. You should try it."

It was like she had cut herself off from all feeling, from everything. From him. *Toradal-shit.*

Riley stared at her as he crossed the room until he was right in her personal space. "Honey, it's going to take a lot more then some little dance to make you forget about me." Cupping her face gently, he gave her a tender kiss, one to stir her senses and keep him firmly at the forefront of her mind.

When she moaned and wrapped her arms around his neck, he knew he'd won her over yet again. Would they ever just make love without fighting first? Lara slid her hands inside his pants and stroked his dick, causing his blood to flame higher and higher. Who cared how it started, as long as it didn't stop.

Backing her against the wall, Riley pressed his chest into hers while he wrestled to get his pants off, still kissing the very life out of her. He wasn't going to leave her any room to clear her mind again. Once the pants were out of the way, he lifted one of her long, gorgeous legs around his waist and ran his hand up to cup her ass. She was naked under his shirt, and somehow that was sexier than any concubine's outfit.

Lara's fingers were doing some exploring of their own, squeezing his shoulder muscles and running up and down his back. She sucked his lip into her mouth and teased it with her tongue, reminding him of when it was his dick in her mouth instead. His fingers drifted of their own violation to her pussy, sinking into the slick wet sheath. She was so hot and wet already, and all he'd done was kiss her.

Kissing her could become a full time job for him.

As he nipped and nibbled his way down her neck, he removed the shirt so he could have unrestricted access to her breasts. Man, how he loved to suck on those nipples. They thrust out at him, pebbled and begging for his touch already. Who was he to say no? Rolling one of the succulent morsels into his mouth, Riley sucked on them forcefully. Lara's hips were thrusting into him, but he wasn't ready to end her torture just yet.

"There's no rush, baby," Riley said against her stomach.

"Speak for yourself!"

"I have something much better to do with my tongue instead." Riley dropped her leg and knelt down in front of her. He speared his tongue into her molten core, tasted her sweet juices and lapped at her nubbin. Apparently Lara was done with conversation as well because she let out a yip of surprise before spreading her legs to provide him better access. She grabbed his head and held it to her clit, as if afraid he'd stop before she was done.

Riley licked faster and her breathing became more labored. His control slipped another notch when he felt the muscles in her legs get tighter in anticipation. As she neared her peak, he stuck his finger in her sheath and rubbed against her hot spot while sucking on her sensitive clit.

Lara's scream of release bounced off the cabin walls, and was music to his ears. Her knees began to buckle, so Riley scooped her up and wrapped her legs around his waist. Her open, weeping pussy was begging for him, even if Lara was beyond speech.

As he sank his dick inside of her, her walls quivered and clenched around him, pulling him deeper and deeper into velvet-lined heaven. Lara moaned weakly into his neck as he plunged in and out of her. He lost all finesse and any control he had when she squeezed him tightly with her inner muscles. He was like a stallion racing to the finish with no thoughts for style points.

As the semen exploded from his body into Lara's, he pushed in as deep as he could go. He wanted to mark her as his, to guarantee no one ever touched her but him. That she never wanted anyone to touch her but him.

The thought scared him so much he almost dropped her lax body to the floor. As it was, he put her down none too gently.

"Sorry, things were getting a little slippery." It was as good an excuse as any.

"No problem, I think I'll go clean up, again. Promise me when we land on the moon base we can have a real cleaning unit."

"We'll see what they have available, but if we ever want to land, I better get back to work."

Riley grabbed his pants off the floor and almost ran back to the cockpit. The tangle of wires he'd left under the console looked a hell of a lot less complicated than his life right about now.

Chapter Eleven

Riley was true to his word and worked all through the night to get the ship fixed enough so they could land. Lara had kept out of his way the best she could. She couldn't do much to help and he seemed to want some space anyway.

She wished she knew what his problem was. It had taken her four tries before she could get calm enough to do her tai chi. For the first time since she'd met Riley, she'd actually had a moment where she'd felt calm, centered, and balanced. Then bam! Riley had to barge in on her and give her the best orgasm imaginable before screwing her brains out against the wall. If that wasn't bad enough, she hadn't even come down to earth yet and he was dropping her like a hot rock and running out of the room.

No wonder she never felt balanced around him, it was like being on an emotional zero-g ride! One minute he was kissing her like she was the most delicious candy in the unit, and the next he was taking off like she offended him or something. Yeah, like anything she could say would get to him. She'd been sarcastic and downright rude to him since she met him and it didn't bother him one bit. Lara couldn't think of anything she could say that would faze him.

Except maybe "I love you".

Wait a second! Where did that thought come from? What the stars was she thinking? There was no sparking way she was falling for some scruffy Flyboy who didn't respect one thing she believed in or stood for. No way, not going to happen.

But what if it already did? What then?

Nothing. There was no future for the two of them. Riley wanted to fly through space unfettered and fancy-free. She had a job, or hoped she still did, and responsibilities. And even if he wouldn't laugh in her face, should she tell him that she lo—cared for him? There was no way they could make a relationship work anyway. Lara had to protect the Emperor, wherever he went, she went. She couldn't expect Riley to wait around for her for months while she traveled around the galaxies going to ribbon cutting ceremonies and politicking.

Besides, they had never once mentioned anything more then wanting one another. It wasn't like they were entering into a life-joining union, or even talked about it. This was physical, pure and simple. A bodily need that had to be taken care of like eating or breathing.

Lara had to keep that foremost in her mind. Riley was not the type of guy who could commit to just one woman, and therefore was not for her no matter how she felt about him. Empress Lisandra might turn a blind eye to her husband's philandering ways, but if Lara ever got married, her husband better not so much as look at another woman.

When had she started thinking about marrying Riley? For that matter, when had she started thinking about marrying anyone? This whole scenario was getting too weird for words. She and Riley were screwing, that's all, nothing else. If she still felt the urge to hitch herself to someone after this adventure was all over with, she'd find some other military brat to tie the knot with. She'd find someone she had something in common with, who shared her ideals and her ways.

And be completely miserable. Just the thought of living with any one of the men she'd met during her career left a bad taste in her mouth. Sure there were a few who she wouldn't mind bedding, but spend the rest of her life with them? Forget it.

Riley leaned his head into the main cabin, startling her out of her dreary thoughts. "We're going to be landing in about twenty minutes, better strap yourself in."

"Okay, I'll be right up." Thank the stars they were finally going to be doing something! With any luck at all they could get this whole fiasco taken care of in another week or two. Of course, all their luck so far had been bad so they'd probably still be chasing their tails a month from now.

Lara smoothed down the dress and slipped on the boots, the blister they had given her was almost healed, but she wouldn't want to have to run in the things. Riley glanced over at her as she walked into the cockpit and buckled herself into the copilot's chair.

"So what's the plan? I mean are we just going to hope they don't recognize the ship, or do we have a backup plan in case we need to leave in a hurry?" She absently picked up Max and began to stroke the humongous cat. He'd become her best friend since she started scratching him behind the ears.

"I don't think we'll have to worry about them recognizing the ship with this big hole in the side. Besides, most folks don't ask many questions as long as you're paying them. We'll see about getting Bonny fixed first, then get ourselves a room. Once we're settled, you lie low and I'll go underground and search for information and a crew."

"And I'm supposed to do what? Sit in the room and watch vids?"

"Remember what happened the last time you insisted on going with me? There was almost an out-and-out riot."

"Would I have to be a concubine here? Seems to me we are across the galaxy from Tramin, I doubt that would be the only role open to me."

"No, but how do you know we won't run into the same problem with someone recognizing you again?"

"I'll take my chances. We're in this together, and I'm not letting you out of my sight until it's over." Lara stared him down. He wasn't ditching her that easily.

"It's your funeral if you're wrong."

"It always has been."

"Fine, hold on. This could be a bumpy landing."

"What else is new?" Everything about Riley had been uneven.

The landing wasn't the roughest Lara had ever encountered, but it was by no means smooth. The fact that Riley could land it at all with a jerry-rigged electrical system and sketchy landing gear made Lara realize he was quite the experienced pilot. His skills would be valued in the Emeraldian Army. He was wasting his talents trolling for space junk.

An idea was beginning to form in her mind, but she pushed it to the backburner for now. She needed to think this through before she said anything.

The moon base was little more than a refueling station for this corner of space. The mechanic who led them into the bay assured them he could fix their ship, for the right price, of course.

"That's galactic robbery!" Riley sputtered as Lara dragged him out of the bay.

"What choice do we have? We can't go anywhere until the hole in the side of the ship is fixed."

"But what he's asking is outrageous! It's extortion!"

"It's supply and demand. We have the demand right now so suck it up and let him do his job. Come on, let's go see if they have some decent rooms in this hole." Lara had been holding Max and her arms were getting tired. When she tried to shift him onto one shoulder, he sprung away and slipped back onto the ship.

"Max!"

"Don't worry about him, he hates to be on land. He'll be happier onboard the ship, and if anyone tries to screw with it, Max will give them a run for their credits."

Lara shrugged her shoulders, if he wasn't worried about his cat she wouldn't be either. Pulling on Riley's arm, she headed off for what looked like an inn. At least she hoped it was. She was tired of being dirty, eating protein bars, and sleeping in a chair. Not that they had done much sleeping of late, but it'd be nice to stretch out on a real bed for a while. Alone.

She needed a little time away from Riley's consuming presence to sort out her wayward thoughts. Maybe the feelings would go away once she had some distance.

Right.

The inn was dim and none too clean. Beer was spilled on the floor, and the place reeked of stale sweat and smoke. The patrons at the bar were few, and seemed very uninterested in Lara and Riley's arrival. Good, the less attention they received the better.

"Go grab a table in the corner, I'll see about getting us some food and a room," Riley directed Lara with a swat on her ass. She arched her eyebrow at his caveman tactics but kept her mouth shut. She'd let him play the big man if it meant she could have some food that didn't come out of a wrapper.

Finding a table that didn't look like it was going to fall apart wasn't easy, but Lara eventually found one in the corner. Stars, this place looked like a meteor had crashed through it. Repeatedly. The tables were dirty and the chairs shaky, and by the angry expression on Riley's face, Lara was willing to bet the service sucked too. Figures. She leaned back carefully and absently tuned into the conversations around her while she waited for Riley to come back.

"I don't care who he is or what he's done, it ain't right to kill a man in cold blood."

"Would you keep it down! What, do you want everyone on the moon to know what we're doing?"

"I don't give a flying *feck* who knows. I won't be a part of murder. Roughing someone up is one thing, killing him because of some piece of fluff's ambition is another. You'll have to find someone else to do it."

"I can't! You're the only one who has a ship and crew to get us out if there's a double cross. I don't trust those Traminians, they're too quiet."

"You'd do better to listen to what they're not saying, why can't they kill this feller themselves? I bet they want to pin it on someone, and that someone is you. It sure won't be me. I'm taking my crew and shoving off at first light tomorrow."

Lara's pulse jumped in her veins! They had to be talking about the Emperor! The two men were arguing now with their heads together so she couldn't hear what they were saying, but she didn't need any further proof. Where was Riley? She needed to tell him about this before these guys took off.

She looked up to where Riley had been waiting for service at the bar, but he'd disappeared while she'd been engrossed in the conversation next to her. Bending over to fiddle with her boot, she stole a glance at the men.

The man who was vehemently arguing against killing her boss was a bear of a man. He had a full head of shaggy brown hair gone mostly gray, and had shoulders as wide as the table. His huge hands made the mug of syntho-beer he was drinking look like a shot glass.

The second man who was pleading with the bear was smaller, thin, and wiry. He was twitching nervously and jumped like a mouse in a room full of cats every time the bear would raise his voice. Lara watched his hand repeatedly stray to the pocket on his calf, then go back to the mug of syntho-beer he was clutching. He had beady little eyes and reminded Lara of a weasel, sleek, nervous, and not to be trusted.

The bear slammed his hands loudly on the table. "I said no, and that's the only answer I'll be giving you. Good day!" His chair went back with a clamor as he stood up and stalked out of the bar.

Lara searched furiously for Riley. What was he doing? Testing the bed out with some willing chambermaid? Her mind worked furiously. Should she follow the bear or wait for Riley to return? If she waited too long she might miss her chance at getting some information about where they were holding the Emperor. If she followed the bear without telling Riley, he'd have a flying fit.

The weasel got up and walked after the bear as soon as he paid the bill, making Lara's decision for her. She wasn't about to lose the only lead they'd gotten.

Lara dashed after the weasel after one last look around for Riley. Spark him! He was going to be mad at her and it was all his fault for disappearing on her in the first place. She burst out of the inn and searched for the weasel. He'd disappeared into thin air! He had to be around here somewhere!

As Lara jogged down the street in her high-heeled boots, her blister rubbed open, making her limp. Just one more mark against Riley. When she saw him again, she was going to rip him up one side and down the other. She was plotting her speech when she heard voices coming from the alley next to the inn. Slowing down she walked as quietly as she could to the mouth of the dim alley.

"Now, Roy, there's no reason to take this personally, it was only a business decision. No need to do anything rash." The bear had his hands up, facing her. The weasel had his back to her, but she could tell by his stance he was holding a weapon on the bear. Probably a laser, something he could use from long distance. He wouldn't want to get close enough to risk a hand-to-hand confrontation.

"This is just a business decision too. I can't have you flying off and telling everyone our plans to kill the Emperor now, can I?"

"I'm no blabbermouth. If you want to murder a man who's done you no wrong that's your business. I'm not your conscience."

"No, you're not, but I still can't take any chances. I'm sorry, Luther, you were a decent guy, and a great pilot but business is business. I'll take good care of your crew for you, at least until after they do their job."

"Not my crew! You can't kill them all!"

Lara had to do something! She had no weapon, no backup, and was facing an unknown opponent. Think! What tools did she have available to her?

Duh? Shock and surprise. Dressed like a hooker, no one would suspect a thing. She hoped.

"Hey boys, either of you looking for a date for the evening?" Lara strutted in, doing her best not to wince each time the boot rubbed her blister a bit more.

"No, lady, we're not looking for any company. Go on, get out of here," the weasel said, taking his eyes off the bear for a brief second. Lara continued walking until she was with in striking distance.

"Come on, sugar, you look like you could use a little lovin'."

"I said no, now scram!"

"Well, you don't have to be rude about it." Lara waited until he turned away from her. As soon as his attention was back on the bear, she snapped out a kick to his wrist, sending the laser flying. That was all the opening the bear needed. He rushed in and picked the weasel up in a bear hug, squeezing the breath out of him with a whoosh.

Lara fumbled for the fallen laser while the bear slammed the weasel's head against the alley wall. As she watched, the bear gave him two more thumps and dropped him to the ground like so much space purge.

"Why thank you, Ma'am. I think I might be interested in a little of that loving now." He looked her over with a gleam in his eye. Lara couldn't believe one minute he was smashing some guy to smithereens, and now he was looking to get laid. Were all males this enslaved to their cocks?

"She's going to be a little too busy to give anyone loving." Riley was standing at the mouth of the alley with another man who was dressed in a slightly tattered uniform.

"Hey, I saw her first. Besides, she offered."

"Well, she can just retract the offer, right Lara?"

"I was just trying to cause a distraction, you can calm down." Was Riley feeling jealous or just mad? The thought of him getting jealous gave her a warm and cozy feeling inside.

"And quite a distraction it was. Because of your timely arrival, I'll live to fight another day. No thanks to that waste of cargo room over there. What do you have to say for yourself, man?" Luther seemed to be talking to the man standing next to Riley. "Go on, Mr. Lub, tell me why I shouldn't bust you down to private for dereliction of duty."

Mr. Lub took a deep breath before speaking. "Captain, I was watching your back when I heard this chap asking questions about Traminians and stuff. He was looking to hire on some hands, and I thought since we weren't going to take the other job, maybe this would be a good chance to make some money. He and I got to talking, then we saw the lady here follow Mr. Roy out of the inn so we followed. Sir."

Luther processed the nervous crewman's speech for a tense minute or two before throwing his hands up and muttering something about getting good help. "Well, if you're looking to hire on a crew, I've got the best in this quadrant, but we ain't cheap, and we don't murder anyone."

"Why don't we retire to the inn and discuss some terms?" Riley offered before Lara could say anything.

* * * * *

He was holding his temper in check by the smallest of degrees and if she so much as raised one of her eyebrows at him, he was going to throw her over his shoulder and carry her to the room. He didn't know if he'd beat the life out of her or screw it out of her, but she wouldn't be walking either way.

Lara must have sensed his mood because she calmly followed his direction without one of her usual smart-ass comments. They'd have it out later, for now he wanted to see what this Luther fellow had for crew and supplies before they made any deals.

"Mr. Lub, see about removing this piece of filth from the alley, then join us in the back room. I think I want a bit more privacy for my business dealings this time around."

"Yes, Sir!"

Luther spoke with the innkeeper and they were quickly escorted to a room at the back of the inn. It was surprisingly clean and well lit. Dishes of food were brought to them carrying succulent stews, piping hot loaves of bread, and crisp greens. Riley stared at the bounty, stunned.

"Where did all of this come from?"

"The kitchen, where do you think?" Luther answered, spooning up some stew.

"Which kitchen? This is a whole lot better than the swill they were serving in the main room. And this room is clean as an Imperial ballroom. What's going on?"

"Well, the innkeeper and I go way back. He reserves this room for his special guests, the ones he doesn't want to piss off. The rest of the place is for the tourists and those unlucky enough to get stuck out here."

"I see. Since this is the only joint on base he can serve cut-rate syntho-beer and food at exorbitant prices."

"I wouldn't go that far. He's just taking advantage of a natural market."

He was taking advantage of something all right. Screw it, they weren't going to be on the base that long, what difference did it make if this guy cheated everyone in sight, there was nothing Riley could do about it.

Riley waited until the servers had left before he began outlining the problems they were facing.

"You don't ask for a little thing now, do you?" Luther leaned back in his chair with a belch.

"If you're not up to the challenge, just say the word and I'll look for someone else." Riley laced his hands behind his head and leaned back as well.

Lara was playing with some food on her plate and keeping her mouth shut. It was what he wanted, but not what he'd expected. It made him nervous as hell. What was she up to?

"I didn't say I couldn't do it. It's just going to take a bit of planning if we want to get your boyo out of there alive. And it's going to have to be quick."

"What kind of planning? And how quick?"

"Roy, that walking piece of space-waste, is looking to hire a crew to kill the Emperor for the Traminians to make it look like a disgruntled tribe offed him. Who knows how many other free agents those Traminians have contacted to do the same? They don't care who offs the guy, as long as they don't get blamed for it."

"What does the compound look like? Do you know anything about the number of guards there are? Where he is being held?"

"I only know what Roy told me, and that is the squad leader wants it to look like the guards have been overpowered, like it was an accident. Roy was going to arrange it with the leader."

"So why did he want you to do it?" Riley pushed away from the table and eyed Luther.

"I guess Roy didn't trust the Traminians not to kill him once the job was done. He wanted someone with a ship that could get them out of there."

"He was probably right to be worried. If you are going to kill an Emperor, you don't want to leave any loose ends lying around. Do you know how to get in touch with the squad leader?"

"Maybe. What do you have in mind?" There was a gleam in Luther's eye that indicated he was thinking what Riley was thinking.

"You call the leader, say Roy filled you in and you were taking the job. We go down grab the Emperor just like it was the original plan, only we say we're taking him off the base to kill him."

"And instead, we hightail it out of there and hit the hyperdrive."

"Exactly."

"Don't you think that's a little too simple? I mean, don't you think they have provisions for something like that happening? If it was my squad I wouldn't take anyone's word but the guy I had already had dealings with." Lara pushed away from the table and leaned down, her breasts swaying in the low-cut dress.

"The fewer the complications, the fewer things can go wrong. Trust me, everything will go just fine." Riley tried to force his attention away from the display of her breasts and focus on the plan.

"What have I said about you saying that to me?"

Chapter Twelve

Lara had left the room while the men were still scheming and plotting. It wasn't like her to leave a planning session, but they seemed to be doing more drinking than planning so she didn't think she was missing much. She slipped off her dress and slid between clean sheets with a sigh. Stars it felt good to be in an honest to goodness bed for a change. *Thank you, Luther!* A couple words from him and the innkeeper suddenly found better accommodations for them. Guess it paid to know the right people!

Things seemed so different now. She was used to making all the decisions; instead she'd been following Riley's lead. As much as she hated to admit it, for the most part he was damn good. Okay, so it wasn't the way she would have done it, but he managed to get them within reach of the Emperor. Not bad for a space scavenger.

Except he was so much more than a space scavenger. He was smart, skilled, and had a tactical mind that was wasted flying through space collecting junk. Punching the pillow flat, Lara rolled over and tried to get into a more comfortable position. The bed seemed too big, too empty.

Best get those thoughts out of your head.

After watching him with Luther, Lara realized Riley liked living life on the edge. He might be a great leader, but he was no longer a team player. She had toyed with the idea of seeing if she could get him to join Emeraldia's army. There was a chance if she pulled the right strings she could get him a decent commission. One that would bring him near her on a regular basis at least. As she watched Riley's eyes light up at the thought of grabbing the Emperor under the Traminians' noses, she saw her hopes go down a black hole.

Riley liked living on the edge and being his own man. There was no way he could fit himself back into the mold of soldier. Even for her.

Flopping back over on the other side, Lara tried to stop the ache that was spreading through her chest. She had been so focused on getting the Emperor back and saving her butt, she hadn't thought about what she'd feel like when everything was done. A tear leaked out of the corner of her eye. Why was she sniveling? She was getting what she wanted, wasn't she? In a couple of days the Emperor would be safe, they'd find out who was behind the kidnapping, and she'd be back home.

Except she didn't really have a home.

What did she have? She'd been part of the military family all her life, but did she really have a family? She had a bank account collecting her pay and that was about it. Big deal. Maybe it was time she started a family of her own, bought a little place on some planet somewhere and settled down.

What was she thinking? Did she think Riley was going to settle down with her once all this was over? Did she want him to?

Throwing her arm over her eyes she tried to force herself to sleep. That was what she needed, a good sleep to help her get her priorities straightened out. Things had been way too unsettled lately and it was scrambling her brains. Everything would be fine when this was all done. She'd have it no other way.

* * * * *

Lara woke from an unsettled sleep when she felt the soft brush of hair against her naked thigh. High up on the inside of her naked thigh.

"What?" She opened her eyes sleepily to see Riley's smiling eyes looking at her from between her spread legs. She must have been dead to the world to have not woken up when he came in the room. "What are you doing?"

"If you don't know, I must be doing it wrong." Riley gave her another devilish smile then dove down into her already dripping core. His tongue trailed along her swollen outer lips as he inserted his finger in between her slick walls.

Fire spread out from the heat of his breath to singe every nerve ending in her body. She was wide awake now all right. Her hips thrust into him, urging him without words to suck her nub, but he continued to torment her by going all around her pleasure spot without touching it.

"What do you want, Lara?"

"Touch me!"

"What else?" Riley rubbed harder inside her. He was hitting her hot spots, but only enough to tease her. Every time she got close to the edge he pulled her back.

"Lick me!"

Riley licked all the way around her, slipped his tongue inside her and licked under the hood of her clitoris this time.

"Who do you want, Lara?" He blew hot breath over her dripping pussy.

"You damn it! You!"

"That's what I wanted to hear." Riley sucked her clit into his mouth and continued to drive his finger into her furiously. She was headed into free-fall and couldn't stop even if she wanted to. Wave after wave of pleasure spiraled through her system, taking every ounce of strength from her.

"I don't think I have a bone left in my body," Lara murmured as Riley kissed his way up her torso to play with her breasts.

"You will shortly."

"Promises, promises," Lara laughed weakly.

"I always live up to my promises; you should know that by now." Riley looked at her intently, his sandy hair hanging down and framing his beautiful green eyes.

"Shut up and fuck me, Riley." This must be it; this would be the last time they made love, that's why he was acting so weird. Lara didn't want to think about it, she just wanted to escape into the dark pool of feeling Riley could provide.

"No."

"No?"

"No. I'm not going to fuck you. I'm going to make love to you until you can't take it anymore."

"I can take a lot."

"Then I'll make love to you until I can't take it anymore."

Riley kissed her face tenderly, sucking gently on her neck, licking the shell of her ear. His touch was so gentle she thought she might cry again, but pushed the thickness in her chest away. The feel of his huge hands on her body was building up the fire once again. Her blood was boiling in her veins and Riley was igniting flash fires wherever he touched.

Running her fingers through his hair, she pulled his mouth to hers. She kissed him with all the pent-up feelings she had no words for, and wouldn't utter even if she did. Running her fingers down his back, she scraped her nails down the muscular expanse until she could grab his butt. Arching her hips, she rubbed her soaking wet pussy against his rigid cock, and tried to pull him into her.

"Not yet."

"Don't play games now, I want you too badly."

"I'm yours." He rubbed the head of his cock against her entrance, spearing her just enough to make her relax. "You just have to tell me you're mine."

"What?"

"Say the words, Lara. Tell me you're mine and only mine." He slipped a little deeper into her, then pulled all the way out when she instinctively arched up.

He was dead serious. His eyes were burning into hers with emotions she was afraid to read.

"Say it!" Riley rubbed his length along her clit, sending sparks of pleasure shooting out. He was so close to her. So damn close, and he wouldn't go in. "You're mine, Lara, you always have been." Again, he dipped in only to back out before she could capture his length.

She was boiling hot and so needy, so very, very needy. Could she speak the words out loud that she couldn't even whisper in her heart? Another searing stroke of his dick against her cleft helped to make up her mind.

"I'm yours. And you're mine. Stars help us."

Riley filled her with a roar of satisfaction that must have wakened every soul in the inn. His hips pumped furiously, slamming her into the soft mattress. Lara braced her heels and pistoned her hips to match his rhythm. It was coming too fast. The explosion was too strong, too intense, and was building so fast she'd never survive it.

"I'm dying!" Lara could do nothing more than hold onto Riley's butt as he jack-hammered into her, scattering her into a million pieces amongst the stars.

* * * * *

Riley knew the second Lara came and thanked anyone who was listening. He didn't know if he could have held on one more second. Her hot wet muscles were gripping him like a fist, and he couldn't stop the force that shot his load into her womb, shuddering with the intensity of it.

Lara's eyes were shinning brightly as she clutched him to her chest. It was almost like she was sensing the end was near as well. He wished she'd never let him go. And it scared the blazes out of him.

Rolling over without a word, Riley held her against him and tucked her head under his chin. There'd be time to talk about the plan he and Luther had devised later, right now he just wanted to savor the feel of her silky skin next to his, and the scent of her in his every breath.

* * * * *

There was something to be said about knowing the right people. Luther had not only gotten them a clean room, but he was making arrangements for Bonny to get the special treatment at the repair shop. She'd be up and ready in two days, which gave them plenty of time to rest and recuperate from their adventures.

Riley met with the rest of Luther's crew and checked out his ship. Luther's crew was made up of assorted misfits and riffraff, but they seemed loyal to the bone to Luther, and that was all that mattered. Lara had trailed along because Luther said it wasn't safe for a female to be left unattended at the inn. In reality, Riley wanted her input on Luther's crew. Men would do a lot of stupid stuff to impress a woman as gorgeous as Lara; little did they know that she could easily take out any one of them without breaking a sweat.

As Bonny got her upgrade, Riley and Luther worked out the nitty-gritty of their plan to rescue the Emperor. Luther would be the front man; he'd already talked to the squad leader about when he was coming to deal with the little problem they'd been experiencing. It would be up to Riley to make sure the Emperor, and Lara, got out alive.

The thought of Lara getting killed trying to rescue the Emperor on her own gave Riley panic attacks. He was tempted to knock her out and tie her up so she couldn't get hurt, but he knew she'd find a way of joining them anyway. Better to let her be a part of it and keep her under his protection than wondering when she was going to show up and get herself shot.

The closer they got to rescuing her Emperor, the more he could see her trying to pull away from him. And he didn't like it one bit. Ever since he made her admit she was his, she'd been unusually quiet. He didn't regret forcing the admission out of her at all. She *was* his and she could fight it all she wanted but that wasn't going to change facts. If they made it through this fiasco of a rescue alive, he was going to see to it that she admitted a hell of a lot more not only to him, but to herself, too.

Riley was checking out the work that had been done on Bonny's electrical system when he caught a whiff of Lara's unique fragrance. Peeking out from under the console he could see her long legs strapped into the sexy boots he'd found for her. His body recognized hers anywhere and began to react almost immediately.

"How's it look?" Lara knelt down between his legs, her hands on his thighs.

"Uh, good. The guy knows his way around a ship all right. Even if he does charge an arm and a leg. What are you doing?" He began sweating as she undid his pants. What was the little minx up to?

He tried to slide out from under the console, but she wouldn't let him.

"Oh, nothing much, just playing. Lift your hips a little please."

Riley bit back a groan as the cool air touched his raging hot dick. Nothing could prevent the one that came out when her hot breath touched his balls, though. He couldn't see what she was doing, but he could feel her hands stroking his length, her mouth sucking first one ball, then the other into the hot wet cavern of her mouth.

Lara released his sack and rubbed her face against it, her silky hair brushed over him in a whisper of a caress. Her hot mouth descended upon his thrumming erection with painful slowness, giving him pain and pleasure by inches.

"You're killing me," he groaned as she took him all the way in. She used her hands to help pump up and down his shaft, drawing every last nuance of feeling out of his tightly wound body.

"Come for me, Riley. I want to make you see the stars!" she said as she came up for air, then swooped back down him in a rush.

Her hot words were all he needed to release the dam of semen that was ready to burst through his body with or without her permission. His hips bucked and his body shook as she sucked every drop out of him.

"I can die a happy man now."

"Don't talk like that! No one is going to die!" Lara got up, enabling Riley to slide slowly out from under the console.

"It was just an expression, baby, calm down."

"Well, there's no need to borrow trouble." Lara paced around the cockpit, and Riley couldn't help but appreciate the way she filled out the dress. She'd taken to wearing her hair down, and the thick mass of it had a life of its own, swirling around her ass like a living thing.

"Everything will be fine, don't you trust me?"

"I trust you; it's everyone else I don't trust."

Riley felt his heart swell in his chest. Not only had she touched him without him having to drag it out of her, but she actually admitted to trusting him for the first time since he'd met her.

"Me either, that's why I insisted we go in separately, and with Bonny fully repaired. I have a backup plan just in case, don't worry."

"I always worry, that's what makes me a good leader. The devil is in the details you know."

"I know, but that isn't what makes you a good leader. What makes you good is that you care about your job, you're determined, and you know your stuff. Those are qualities that will take you anywhere you want to go, and not just in the military either."

"What are you trying to say?"

He ran a hand through his hair. What was he trying to say? "I've been doing some thinking since all this began. You're wasted in the military. They don't give a shit about you, only that you are willing to bust your ass for a few kernels of attention and the occasional promotion. If you were in the civilian workplace, you'd be a valued businessperson. In the military, you are just one more cog in their wheel."

"You don't know what you are talking about. I would be begging on the streets if it weren't for the military. They've given me everything I've ever had. They're the only family I've got."

"Yeah, well I—"

"Hey, you ready to check out the modifications to the artillery?" one of the service techs called into the ship.

"Be right there," Riley called down, fastening up his pants.

"We'll talk about this again, Flyboy."

"You got it, Sweet Cheeks." Riley slapped her quickly on the ass on his way out. It was nice to get the last word in for once.

He quickly forgot about the discussion though once he got a look at the repairs that had been made to Bonny. Riley let out a low whistle between his teeth when he saw the gleaming new cannons mounted in the rear of the ship.

"*Feck*! Where'd you get your hands on those?" he asked the tech.

"A beat-up Traminian fighter got sucked into the moon's gravitational pull, and I just happened to be lucky enough to grab it."

Riley didn't voice his thought that maybe the fighter had a little help getting beat up. Finders-keepers he always said.

"Want to see the rest of the modifications? She should be ready to go by tomorrow."

"Tomorrow, that's perfect. Yeah, what else have you done to my baby?"

"You haven't let this renegade touch Lara have you?" Luther asked with a booming laugh, walking up to them.

"Nope, but I let him touch Bonny, which is just as precious to me." Riley could have bitten out his tongue as soon as the words were out of his mouth. Guys just didn't say stuff like that to other guys in his world.

"Never put a ship above the love of a good woman, my boy. I know from experience you can always replace a ship, but once you lose the love of a woman it's gone for good."

The service tech looked decidedly uncomfortable with all this talk of love. "Do you want to see the new stuff or not?"

"Absolutely. Let's see what you've done!" Luther boomed.

Riley trailed along in Luther's wake, ohhing and ahhing over every new gun, security device, and comfort that had been installed. His mind was only half on the improvements though. He couldn't stop Luther's words from running over and over again through his mind.

Did he love Lara? Did she love him? He'd never thought too much about that namby-pamby emotion before, but strange feelings seemed to be popping out all over the place. First he made Lara admit that she belonged to him, then he said she was as precious to him as his ship, now Luther was talking about the love of a good woman like they were discussing ion blasters or some other normal topic. What the hell was going on here?

Pushing those thoughts to the back of his mind, Riley forced himself to concentrate on the work that had been done to Bonny. He'd worry about what was happening between him and Lara later. There'd be plenty of time to straighten out all of this emotional garbage after they rescued the Emperor.

Chapter Thirteen

"Okay, so you know the drill?"

"You've only gone over it with me a million times. I'm not stupid, you know. I have actually been in a few battles myself before." If he asked her one more stupid question she was going to strangle him! She outranked him for stars' sake! She'd been leading military operations for years.

"You may have fought before, but I doubt you have much covert operations experience. Enough shit is going to go down that I can't control, I want to control all the factors I can." Riley ran his hand through his sandy hair and tapped his fingers on the console.

"Fine. Luther is going to land his ship smack-dab in the middle of the compound. He and his crew are going to stomp around and pretend like they are fighting the skeleton crew of Traminians that are there."

"Hopefully it's a skeleton crew."

"Yeah, well, that's one of those things you can't control. Anyway, while he's doing that, we take advantage of the diversion and land in the back near the prison where they are hiding the Emperor. You'll take front guard, and I'm in charge of Touchy Thomellt. We grab him and haul his fat ass to Bonny and take off for Emeraldia like our pants are on fire."

"And Luther and his crew follow us, receiving their pardons upon landing."

"That's one of those things *I* can't control."

"But I'm sure your boss will be more than happy to cooperate after we explain to him what happened with his wife and ally."

"We'll see."

That was only one part of the plan that had Lara nervous. Riley had promised Luther and his crew that if they agreed to help out, the Emperor could grant them pardons for their extracurricular activities. Most of them were pretty minor, a little smuggling, a couple of bar fights that got way out of hand. Luther, on the other hand, was wanted on four planets for stealing the ship he now used for smuggling and other jobs Lara wanted to know nothing about.

If only he hadn't stolen it from Thomellt's cousin. That could prove to be a bit tricky. Well that, and the reason he stole it in the first place was to escape the palace guards who were chasing him after catching him in bed with said cousin's wife.

Yeah, 'cause that was going to be easy to explain.

Strapping the laser Riley had procured for her to her thigh, she tested her mobility in the dress and boots. Man, she couldn't wait to get back into a uniform, even if it was nothing more than a souped-up body stocking. Lara warmed up and stretched a bit to ease the nervous butterflies that were fluttering in her stomach. She wanted to be loose and limber in case they had to fight their way back to the ship.

She was sure they were going to have to do some fighting, no matter what Luther said.

"If anything goes bad, grab the Emperor and hightail it out of here on Bonny. I'll follow with Luther."

"I can't fly Bonny! I can barely fly a speedster." Nothing was going to go so wrong. He was talking about if he got killed, that would be the only thing that could keep him away from his ship.

"She can fly herself for the most part; she just needs you to start her up."

"I'm not leaving without you." The very thought made the butterflies in her stomach sink like lead weights.

"Then you aren't getting off the ship."

"What are you talking about?"

"I am not letting you risk everything without knowing you'll take care of yourself first. If I can't trust you to follow directions I'll handcuff you to the brand-new bed and leave you here."

"Like hell you will!"

"Then promise me you'll follow orders without question. That's your motto, isn't it? This is a military operation and I need you to show me what a good little soldier you are. Your job is to protect the Emperor, not me. You can't protect him if you're preoccupied with me. Make sure you get him out of there and back to Emeraldia before his idiot wife blows the whole galaxy to space dust."

Damn it! Why did he have to put it that way? He was manipulating her with her own rhetoric. When did he become more important than her job? How did he suddenly take number one priority? And why did this bomb of an epiphany have to drop on her now?

"Well, what's it going to be? Are you going to follow orders or play out my secret bondage fantasy? I'm kind of hoping you'll fight me on this one, actually."

"Bite me, Riley. I'll play it your way, but you had better watch your ass."

"But yours is so much nicer."

"Riley!"

"Just kidding. I don't expect anything to go wrong; I'm only planning for it just in case. Now buckle up, we're going to have to draft off that tub Luther flies to get in without setting off any alarms. It may get a little bumpy."

"What a surprise."

Lara waited with clenched fingers while Riley powered Bonny down. They were operating on the minimum amount of power, using the vacuum of air created by Luther's ship to pull them along. Riley had been sure that the monitors the Traminians used wouldn't be able to pick them up as long as they stayed close to Luther. Once they landed, the Traminians would be too busy "fighting" to worry about them. Hopefully.

There were an awful lot of blank holes in this plan, and they made Lara damn nervous. The lights in the ship dimmed as Riley continued to shut down the power. When only the life-support functions were on, he sat back with a grunt. She was surprised when he reached over and grabbed her clenched hands and rubbed his thumb in soothing circles.

"Everything will be fine, baby. Don't worry, I won't let anything happen to your Emperor."

"It's not him I'm worried about." Lara didn't even know if Riley heard her, because his attention was snagged by the turbulence shaking them. He needed both hands to control Bonny and keep her under the cloak of Luther's ship.

"Luther's getting ready to land, hold on, we're going to break off in ten seconds."

Lara counted down in her head and waited. She was only down to three when Riley slammed on the throttles and sped off under the dust cloud created by Luther's landing. Riley was all business now. Steering the ship, he eased her down behind some outbuildings in the rear of the compound. Lara could see soldiers scurrying like ants to the courtyard where Luther's crew was blasting lasers for all they were worth.

"Soon as I open the doors, you run for the building at ten o'clock. I'll cover you."

"I know the drill, you do your job, I'll do mine." Lara snapped herself into her own business mode and prepared for the mission.

"It's showtime!"

* * * * *

Riley watched as Lara scampered to the building, dove for cover, and then signaled the all-clear sign. He was doing his best to push everything out of his head except the job, but it wasn't easy. Letting her out of the ship was the hardest thing he had ever done in his life.

He took a deep breath, then bolted for the building. The shed housed what looked like an unmanned surface-to-air laser inside. Probably some sort of artillery shed.

"He's in one of those two buildings, you take the one on the left, I'll go right," Lara ordered.

"Yes, Ma'am." He was pretty sure the Emperor was on the left anyway.

"On three, one—"

"Two, three, go!" Riley ran out first, hoping to draw any fire, but there was none. He refused to look at her one more time to see if she made it to cover or not. At this point the best thing he could do for her was his job without screwing up by worrying over her.

The building he'd hit was indeed a prison, but the only thing it was holding were casks of wine and beer. Looked like the boys had been busy as several of the casks were empty already. Riley took a look around for any guards, but the only evidence there had even been someone in the building was a pile of what looked to be vomit in the corner.

Jogging into the hallway, Riley searched for a way to get to Lara's side. There were three passageways. The one on the left was the one he took to get in here. The one on the right probably led to the courtyard, so that left the center one.

He had taken two steps towards it when he heard the familiar sounds of laser fire and Traminian swearing. Yup, he'd found Lara. Tearing ass down the passageway, Riley pulled his gun and prepared to shoot his former brothers in arms. It hadn't escaped his attention that any one of these soldiers could be a former squad member or someone he'd trained.

Lara was crouched in a corner behind some boxes, firing at three soldiers. She had to stop occasionally to push some fat turd he assumed was the Emperor back into the corner.

Stupid ass, couldn't he just sit there and be still, did he want to get her killed? Riley shot over the heads of the three soldiers. If he could get them into the cell he wouldn't have to kill them.

"Get them into the cell and get the hell out of here!" Riley shouted to her, diving for cover behind a chair.

"The cell doesn't even lock!" she shouted back.

"What the hell?"

"Captain Riley? Is that you? Hold your fire!" The soldier who seemed to be in charge put up his weapon and made the other two do the same.

Riley searched his memory. The red hair reminded him of a wet behind the ears probie he had trained, but this guy couldn't be him. Could it? "Red? Is that you?"

"Yes, Sir. I made Lieutenant shortly after you, ah, left."

"Got kicked out you mean. Well, good for you."

"I don't mean to interrupt this little reunion, but I'd like to get out of here." Lara stood up. She'd stopped firing, but still held her weapon at the ready.

"Take him and go. We didn't want any part in kidnapping and killing an Emperor. That's what we were trying to tell you when Jol here accidentally fired on you."

"What do you mean? What is going on?"

"We have been following orders up to this point, but when it came to killing royalty, well, me and the boys had a discussion about that. We don't want to lose our jobs and put our families at risk, but we ain't murderers."

Shit, what now? If he left them here to take the rap for letting the Emperor go, they could get court-martialed. There was no choice; he had to bring them along. When had he become such a freaking hero? "Okay, you three go with Lara and the Emperor. I'll take rear guard. Go!"

Lara looked at him incredulously, but took off running, dragging the slobbering idiot behind her. The three Traminians followed her at a run while Riley kept watch over their backs.

They had almost made it to the ship when all hell broke loose.

A Traminian fighter ship flew overhead, shooting laser blasts at the crew, and scattering them like so many marbles from a careless child's hand.

"Go! Go!" Riley ran to the artillery shed they had hidden behind when they landed and grabbed the surface-to-air laser, shooting wildly until he got the feel for the gun.

Lara dragged one of the soldiers up the ramp to Bonny while looking around for him. Red pushed the Emperor into the ship and the other crewmember ran to help Lara bring their wounded companion to safety.

Once Riley knew she was safe, he focused on buying them some time to get out of there. A flash of pain in his shoulder brought Riley's attention around to a squad coming from the courtyard. He aimed some laser fire at them and went back to keeping the ship off Lara's back.

He'd scored a shot at the fuel tank that should take care of the ship when another squad rounded the building. Lara and the mutinying crew were aiming fire at them so Riley turned his sights on the first group. The laser wasn't very accurate for land battles, but it was powerful enough to make up for it.

"Get out of here! I'll cover your ass! Go! That's an order!" Riley shouted at Red. He knew Lara wasn't going to follow his orders. "Get her ass on the ship and move out! Now!" He blanketed the area with fire to buy them time. His shoulder burned like blazes from the shot he took, but he didn't care. The only thing that was important was getting Lara to safety; he'd worry about himself later.

When the ground rumbled from Bonny's takeoff, Riley thought he'd faint in relief. Another shot at his head reminded him he had to worry about his own safety now.

* * * * *

Lara swore at the radio and slammed her hand down in frustration. She had no idea if Luther knew Riley was still on the base or not. Either Luther's radio had been shot or there was no one left to answer it. If Luther left Riley stranded on that planet, so help her, she'd go back and get him herself. She had been stalling their entry into hyperdrive until she made contact, but she was running out of time. Once in hyperdrive, they would be cut off from any communications from Luther's ship, and Lara couldn't take that step yet.

"Major, the Emperor would like to speak with you," Red told her, looking a little wild around the eyes. She had threatened to cut his balls off and feed them to him when he dragged her onto the ship and took off without Riley, so she guessed he had cause.

"Relax, Lieutenant, I'm not going to hurt you. I know you were following orders, which is what I should have done in the first place. You did your job and I won't take out my anger on you."

"Thank you Ma'am, I appreciate that." He issued a crisp salute and turned on his heel.

Lara got up and headed reluctantly for the sleeping cabin. The Emperor had taken it over as his own personal quarters upon their arrival. She hoped he didn't expect her to share it with him. There was no way she was in the mood for playing touchy-feely right now.

"You wanted to see me, Sire?" Lara said as blankly as possible.

"Yes, Major McDaniel. I wished to thank you for your bravery."

"All part of my job, Sire."

"Yes, I know. And after learning of my wife's treachery, I no longer hold you responsible for letting me be kidnapped in the first place. Although I will expect you to take precautions in the future that something like this won't occur again."

If you had waited to let me test the meat as thoroughly as I'd asked, you fat slob, none of this would have happened. "Of course, Sire. We should be entering hyperdrive shortly, you may wish to go to sleep to avoid the turbulence of the ride." *And the turbulence of my fist in your face if I have to put up with you for much longer.*

The Emperor shuddered in his ratty robes. "I would prefer to remain asleep until we reach civilization again. You may go." He fluttered his hand in her direction while demanding a sleeping shot from Bonny.

"Yes, Sire." *You bloated excuse of humanity.*

There was no use delaying it any longer. The sooner she got the Emperor off her hands, the sooner she could go back and get Riley.

"Bonny, set coordinates for Emeraldia and take us into hyperdrive." Riley had taken the precaution of keying Bonny for Lara's voice. Now she knew why.

Damn him.

"Yes, Major. Entering hyperdrive in thirty seconds, please strap in, Major."

"Don't tell me, it could be a bumpy ride."

Lara strapped herself in and waited for the rush of hyperdrive. As the stars flew past the window, she wished she could run as quickly from the pain that was stabbing her heart.

Chapter Fourteen

"Major, we're approaching Emeraldia. I, ah, think it might be best if you were the one that security saw on the screen." Red twitched nervously.

"Probably a good idea, I'll take the Captain's chair, why don't the three of you lay low for a while, at least until I can explain some things." Do some fast-talking was more like it.

"Would you like me to wake the Emperor?"

Lara thought about it, seriously thought about just leaving him asleep until she could dump the lot of them and turn Bonny around to find Riley, but realized she still had a job to do. She sighed heavily, "I suppose so. But give me another fifteen minutes. I might need him to prove I'm who I say I am, but I don't want to put up with him for a minute longer than I have to."

Red gave her a conspiratorial grin and went below. Lara set Bonny's coordinates for Emeraldia's visitors' landing bay. She'd probably be shot on sight if she tried to land in the military one.

"Emeraldia Station, this is Major Lara McDaniel flying the commandeered vessel *The Donegal*. I have Emperor Thomellt aboard and am requesting permission to land." Lara waited for a picture to come on the vid screen. When a harried-looking control tower dispatcher appeared she had to repeat her message twice before she finally sent for her commanding officer.

"McDaniel! What's this I hear about you flying a ship with the Emperor on it? Report!"

"Colonel Baker, Sir! Following Galaxy by law number 197-42, I commandeered this vessel and proceeded on a rescue mission for the Emperor. With the help of some civilian counterparts and three Traminian soldiers, I was able to rescue the Emperor. He is on board and is readying himself now. Permission to land, Sir!"

There was a hushed consultation behind the colonel and Lara began to sweat. What if they believed the Empress and thought maybe she had something to do with the Emperor's disappearance? She had to remain calm. If she panicked she would look guilty. Focus on the issue at hand, namely the dangerously low fuel levels, and deal with the rest of the crap later.

The discussion was muffled, but Lara finally made out the voice of Colonel Baker, "I don't give a rat's ass what that bitch says. That's my soldier up there and if she says she has the Emperor, then I believe her."

Go Baker!

"Permission to land granted, Major. Stay aboard the ship and don't let anyone, I repeat anyone, in or out until I have debriefed you."

"Yes, Sir!"

There was obviously much more going on here than met the eye. She'd better warn the Emperor after they landed. Gee, that was something to look forward to.

"Bonny, follow the guide beam and bring us in. Once we land, seal the doors until my signal. No one goes in or out."

"Affirmative, Major. Please buckle up for landing."

Max, who'd shown the loyalty of a three-dollar whore, jumped on her lap and kneaded her thighs as Bonny circled the tower to wait for the guide beam. He'd been making the rounds amongst the Traminians who were used to having the cats around.

"Oh, suddenly I'm worthy of your attention again, huh?" Lara said, scratching him around the ears.

The rotund cat just purred and closed his eyes in kitty ecstasy. Lara was about to dump him on the floor to begin the landing sequence when his fur shot up like he'd been electrocuted and his tail shot out.

"Red! Get up here! Man the cannons! Send Jol to the gunner's deck!" Lara took manual control and made a sharp left turn, buzzing a supply drone that was headed into port. No sooner had she cleared the drone than it burst into bits, hit by a blast from a Traminian ion cannon.

"Major! What is going on! I demand an explanation. Your reckless flying made me spill coffee down the front of me." The Emperor waddled to the door of the cockpit, blocking the way for Red to get in. There was no way she could fly this bird herself and man the guns, too; she needed the Lieutenant's help.

"With all due respect, Sire, get your fat ass out of the way so Red can help me or coffee stains will be the least of your worries. We're being shot at by your wife's lover. Get below decks and stay the hell out of the way."

Lara didn't even look to see if he followed her directions, just handed controls of the ship to Red and took over the guns. Weapons were something she could handle, evasive flying maneuvers were not.

"Lieutenant, three ships coming straight on. One of 'em is the Military Commander's cruiser," Jol called through the headphones. A note of fear colored his voice.

"I don't give a shit who it is. Shoot to kill, Private!" If Rody wanted to fight her, then he had better be prepared to die.

Red pulled them up into a loop. Lara took advantage of the angle and fired one of the cannons at the outrider. She assumed the ship at the point of the triangle was Rody's. At least she hoped so because that was where she was headed next.

"Jol, you watch for help coming from Emeraldia, prepare to shoot them on my say-so."

"Ma'am?"

"I don't know whose side they're on, and until I'm sure about their loyalty I want you ready to blow them out of the sky."

The other outrider flew ahead, coming straight at Bonny. It was too close to use an ion cannon, but the guns could do quite a bit of damage. As Red dipped them to the side, Lara aimed her shots at the fuel tank. Her shots hit the ship, but did no damage. As they buzzed by, Jol managed to get a shot of his own in that was dead-on. The second outrider was history too.

Now it was just Bonny versus Rody's cruiser. Suddenly, Bonny seemed very small and slightly overmatched.

"What type of firepower does he have on that thing?" Lara asked Red.

"You name it, he has it. He has shit I don't even think they have names for yet, uh, Ma'am."

"Wonderful. Prepare to fly your heart out."

"Or die trying."

"I really didn't need to hear that," Lara muttered under her breath. Her hands were sweaty, but steady on the controls. Red would do the best he could to get them close enough to fire one, maybe two shots. After that it was up to her and Jol to get those shots in.

It would be like trying to thread a needle on the back of a land cruiser.

"Let me know when we're in range, Bonny."

"We'll be in range in five, four," Bonny's voice counted down calmly.

Before she could get to three, a shot from the cruiser's cannon blasted along the side of the ship, rocking her like a teacup in a rocket wash.

"Shit! Evasive action!"

Red banked the ship as hard as he could, rolling it over when she didn't respond correctly.

"Major, I think he got a piece of the tail, she's not turning right."

"Bonny! Damage report!"

"Heavy damage to the starboard side, the rudder has been lost, Major."

Lara was contemplating a suicide mission on the cruiser when the light from an ion cannon lit up the sky. Help was coming from another quarter. It was Luther's ship! Luther's ship was firing on Rody!

"Hot damn! Luther, I think I could kiss you right about now!" Lara yelled into the communicator.

"I wouldn't mind that a bit darlin' but I know someone who would, and I'd rather not have to fight him when he is done with Rody."

"Riley! You have Riley!"

"That I do, darlin', that I do. Now land that hunk of metal while we make sure old Rody boy gets his day in court."

"Did you hear that, Red? Riley's alive! He's alive and he's in Luther's ship!" Lara didn't care that she was grinning like an idiot, or that tears were streaming down her face. Riley was alive!

"Yes, Ma'am, I heard. Now let's try to keep ourselves alive, too, and land in one piece. Would it offend you if I volunteered to bring us in?"

"Not at all, not at all." Lara didn't care who landed them as long as they touched down and she could see Riley again.

* * * * *

Riley paced the ship impatiently. All communication had been cut off; he didn't know what was going on with Lara. The only thing he knew was he was sealed in Luther's ship until Imperial Command released them.

Rody's ship had been taken in by tractor beam as soon as they got in range of the tower. Riley had just taken the communicator when a Colonel Baker saying all transmissions would be blocked and they would be sealed in the ship until further notice interrupted him.

That had been two days ago. Luther was sweating it out, swearing that they were all going to get strung up and they should blast their way out of the bay. Riley was getting a little sick of hearing the doom and gloom predictions, but as the hours turned into days, he was beginning to believe them against his better judgment. If something didn't break soon, Luther would fight his way out and Riley would never see Lara again.

"Someone's coming up the ramp!" one of the lookouts called.

Riley ran to the vid screen. There were three people walking up the ramp, two of them obviously military, and one person wearing the robes of a Traminian Counselor.

"Colonel Baker of the Imperial Army requesting permission to board!" It didn't sound all that much like a request, but Riley nodded to Luther anyway.

"Permission granted. Welcome aboard the *Sweet Deal*, Colonel Baker."

The party marched into the main cabin and stood at attention while Luther's crew shifted their feet nervously. No one said a word, waiting to see who would break first.

"At ease, gentlemen. We've come here to thank you for your part in rescuing the Emperor. Lieutenant Colonel Scott here has been instructed to issue pardons per Major McDaniel's request. If you'll form a line, Scott will do the necessary paperwork while I speak to Riley."

There were sighs of relief and a few weak cheers as the men gathered around the slender Lieutenant Colonel. Riley watched as the Colonel and the Counselor approached him. What did they want with him?

"Captain Riley? Counselor Grady and I would like to talk to you privately if you have a moment or two to spare."

"I've got nothing but time Colonel Baker, you still have my ship impounded somewhere on this planet."

"That will be taken care of all in due time, Captain Riley."

"Just Riley, Sir. I haven't been a Captain for several years."

"That is one of the things I wanted to discuss with you Riley," the robed Counselor said. His hands fluttered up and down, and he looked appalled at the condition of the ship. His Adam's apple bobbed up and down like a child's yoyo, and Riley found himself oddly fascinated by it.

"Not much to talk about. I lost my command when Rody got his. End of story."

"We'd like to offer you your command back again. Barring that, we'd change your discharge to honorable and you'd receive all of your veteran's benefits."

"Not to mention a sizable reward for your part in rescuing the Emperor and averting a Federated Galaxies crisis," Colonel Baker added.

"Thank you, Sir, Counselor. I'm somewhat overwhelmed. I guess I need to think about it a little before I make up my mind." What was he saying? Here was everything he wanted on a silver *fecking* platter? Whose words were popping out of his mouth?

"Makes sense to think about it a little first, son. I'll see to it your ship is repaired as soon as possible, and that you and your men have land-side accommodations."

"Thanks again, Sir. Can you tell me what happened to the three Traminians that were on Major McDaniel's ship?" He didn't ask about Lara, but he wanted to.

"The Major made sure they were treated like heroes for helping her save the Emperor. They've been cleared in their part of the conspiracy and have agreed to cooperate with Imperial authorities."

"Good."

"Oh, and if you don't want to go back to the Tramin army, I've got plenty of room in my command for someone with your skills."

"I'll think about it." Riley had a hell of a lot more to think about than he'd ever expected.

Chapter Fifteen

Lara had tried to get to see Riley since she heard he had been released, but she hadn't had a minute to call her own since she'd been debriefed. She'd spent an entire day describing each and every action she took from the moment Drog woke her with his call until they landed on Emeraldia.

The Empress was being held in "protective custody" until her trial. She hadn't helped her case any when she was caught trying to steal a flyer with one of her bodyguards and several hundred thousand credits. Too bad she hadn't been smart enough to realize all her transmissions with Rody were easily retrieved. Her case didn't look good. And Lara couldn't be happier.

Even after her debriefing, she had to go over and over the story for the military, the lawyers, and the Counselors from Tramin. She'd tried to paint Riley in as good a light as she could and she stood up for Luther and his crew as well. The Traminians she had brought with her had been taken into custody immediately, but she'd managed to point out the benefits of having their cooperation instead of treating them like criminals.

There would be no time to herself until after she had her meeting with the Emperor. After that, she had another meeting with court officials, and then there was the planet-wide celebration that was being held tonight. Lara could have cared less about the party, but it was being held in her honor and she couldn't very well skip it.

Maybe Riley would be there too? News on him was scarce. Luther and his crew were cutting a big swath through the single ladies, the Traminian soldiers had been hailed as heroes, but she'd heard nothing about Riley. The most she could get out of the service crew was that he'd moved back onto Bonny and was giving them grief over every repair they made.

Probably wanted to get out as soon as possible. Colonel Baker had given her a short version of the conversation he'd had with Riley. It hadn't sounded all that promising.

Well, what else did he want? She'd worked her ass off so that he could get his command back if he wanted it, a big reward, and his ship fixed. He should be bouncing around the place like a lunatic. Instead he was holed up in his ship like some space age hermit. He was back to just his ship, his cat, and his own company.

Fine. If that was what he wanted, so be it. She'd never claimed to have any strings on him. They hadn't made promises to each other. They both knew the deal. People like them weren't meant to have long-term relationships.

Then how come it hurt so badly? Lara took a shuddering breath and got changed into her Class A uniform. Luckily it wasn't a body stocking like her everyday one. Her hair was braided so tightly she would have a headache before the night was over. Hell, she'd have one anyway after dealing with the brouhaha that was going to be running rampant over the planet. Maybe after she did her thing she could slip away to her bunk and get a good night's sleep for a change. She hadn't had one in a long, long time.

Not since the last time she'd made love to Riley.

Stop it!

Lara squared her shoulders and started out on the trek to the Emperor's quarters for her meeting. There was no use crying over what could never be. Or perhaps never was.

As she approached the Emperor's sitting area, the guards opened the doors for her immediately. The Emperor and his heir were sitting on a dais eating fruit. Lara's stomach grumbled audibly, reminding her she hadn't been eating well lately.

"Oh good, Major, you're on time."

"Yes, Sire." She was always on time, what did he want?

"It has come to my attention that We have not been sufficiently grateful for the sacrifices you made for Our rescue."

"I was just doing my job, Sire." She hated it when he used the royal "We", back on the ship when he was tossing his cookies he wasn't so damn full of protocol.

"Very true. And as a reward for such and excellent job, We have decided to offer you the rarest of treasures."

"Honestly, Sire, I need no other reward than your safety." And distance. If he offered to fuck her as a reward she'd run screaming from the room.

"Don't be ridiculous. It is Our privilege to offer suitable rewards to Our subjects, and We wish you to become betrothed to the Heir of the Throne."

"Excuse me?" She couldn't have heard right. Did he just say betrothed to the Heir? She looked over at the seventeen year old who was sitting next to his father, eyeing her with something akin to a kid in a candy store.

A shudder of revulsion tore down her spine before she could control her reaction.

"The announcement will be made tonight at the celebration. Your marriage will take place after a suitable engagement."

"Emperor Thomellt, I am, ah, honored. I don't have words to describe what I am feeling right now. Unfortunately, I must decline. I am really not suited for palace life."

"Don't be ridiculous girl! We are offering you the chance of a lifetime. For a woman of your station to be in the company of the Heir is beyond imagining."

What was he thinking? She was a military brat, she couldn't be a princess! Wait a minute. He said she'd be betrothed to the heir for a period of time, not married. So, during that time he'd get to test out the goods so to speak. Then, when it was convenient for the Emperor, the engagement would be broken and she'd be shuffled off somewhere. He was only doing this as a PR move because the whole planet was sick of paying the price for his excesses. If he'd been paying attention to what had been going on under his nose then his wife never could have started a war. He thought by setting her up with the heir he'd look like he had a feel for the common man.

"I can see the offer has completely taken your wits away. I will wait for you to come to your senses before I bring this up again. You may go."

"Thank you, Sire." *You bet your fat ass I'll go. And I won't be coming back.* Lara kept her face neutral as she walked from the Emperor's quarters to the Judicial Center. She had to give them yet another statement, repeating her story for the umpteenth time. Lara forced her face into a blank mask. She wouldn't let any sign of her inner fury show on her face, but her mind worked overtime.

She had a lot of plans to make, and not a whole lot of time to work with. As soon as she was released from her deposition, she made a stop at the bank, and then at Imperial Headquarters. She couldn't believe after everything she'd done, all she had sacrificed, the Emperor still saw her as nothing more than a pawn in his political game.

Riley was right, she wasn't valued by the military, and she wasn't happy either. This wasn't a life, this was an assembly line, and she was just another cog on the wheel. Well no more. It was time she made a break; she only hoped she wasn't too late.

"Hey Major, you'll be late for your own party! What are you doing here?" The sergeant on duty asked as Lara stormed through the door at Headquarters.

"I'm looking for Colonel Baker, is he in?"

"Yeah, I'll buzz you through." Lara waited for the door to open, tapping her foot impatiently. She was having a hard time controlling her feelings. Her anger had turned to a plan of action, but what if it was the wrong plan?

After being buzzed through she walked briskly down the hallway until she reached the Colonel's door. She rapped sharply and waited for him to open it.

"Major! This is a surprise. Aren't you going to be late for the celebration?"

"I have a little time, Sir."

"What can I do for you?" Colonel Baker leaned back in his chair and motioned for her to sit down.

"Colonel Baker, I've come to tender my resignation from the Imperial Army. My tour of duty has been fulfilled for several weeks, and I have no desire to continue with my present duties. Sir."

The Colonel's feet hit the floor with a thud and his chair toppled backwards as he shot to his feet.

"What are you talking about? You're a *fecking* hero! You can't just quit!"

"Yes, Sir, I can. I have given my entire life to the military, risked my life on numerous occasions only to have all my work and dedication taken for granted."

"This is because of the Emperor's idea to betroth you to his idiot son, isn't it?"

"That is only part of it, Sir. If I may be frank?"

"Why stop now? Go ahead."

"I am thirty years old. I have been in the military my entire life, worked my way up from the orphanages to officer school. It has only been in the last week that I even wore clothes that weren't uniforms. I have no family, no home, and quite honestly, no more desire to risk my life for some fat bastard that can't see me as anything other than a piece of ass or a chess piece. I want a chance to have a life." A life with Riley if she could manage it.

"I guess it's about time. What are you going to do?" the colonel asked.

"I'm going to go see if I can catch a fast ship and explore the worlds around me."

"If you hurry, I bet I know where you can catch one."

"Where?"

"The service bay. *The Donegal* just requested permission to take off. I'll delay the order as long as I can, but you had better hurry."

"Yes, Sir!"

Lara bolted out of the colonel's office, her braid flying behind her like a flag. People dodged out of her path as she went tearing around the corner to the service bay. Riley was standing at the top of the ramp to Bonny, his arms crossed over his chest, his foot tapping.

"Come to see me off?" He gave her a smile that didn't reach his eyes.

"Maybe, maybe not. Maybe I just missed Max?" What if he didn't want her after all? What if she was wrong about these feelings coursing through her? What if she was right and she did love him, but he didn't love her? Suddenly, all the implications of her actions reared up and scared her. She couldn't take another step. There were only ten feet separating her from Riley, but it might as well have been a hundred. She couldn't move.

"Well then, come on up and see him, if you missed him so much."

"I don't want to delay your takeoff." He had been about to leave without saying goodbye. You didn't do that when you loved someone.

"I'm not going far, just to the civilian bay."

"Then you aren't leaving?"

"Without saying goodbye? You don't have a whole lot of faith in me, Sweet Cheeks."

"Let's just say my faith has been a bit shaken these last few days." The ice that had frozen her was melting, and her knees were the first things to turn to water. She took a hesitant step forward, then another and another until she was running up the ramp.

Riley was waiting with open arms, running to meet her halfway. He scooped her up into his arms and carried her into Bonny's main cabin. Lara rained kisses around his face, running her hands over his chest and squeezing her legs around his waist.

Lara tried to speak in between kisses. "I missed you so much. I was so worried; I didn't know what happened to you."

"Ditto! When you didn't come to the ship, I thought maybe you had run away for good."

"No, never think that. I just couldn't get away. I've been in meetings night and day. Stars but that feels good." Riley had undone her uniform and was grasping her breasts like he hadn't seen them in years.

He gave them a longing stare, then reluctantly moved an arm's distance away. "We have to talk first."

"Can't we talk after? I've missed you so much, Riley."

"I've missed you, too. I was moving to the civilian bay so I could leave easily after I kidnapped you tonight. But we need to talk first. A lot has happened since you snatched the Emperor."

"I know. Are you going to take back your command? You are an amazing leader. Red told me how all the probies were terrified of you, yet would give their lives for you, too. He told me about how you saved the entire squad when—"

"I'm sure he told you all sorts of things, but they don't matter. I'm not taking the commission."

"You're not? But I thought that was so important to you?"

"It was, once. I'm not taking the reward money either."

"Like hell! I had to bust my ass to get you that money; you sparking well better take it!" What did he mean it wasn't important to him anymore?

"I'll take it only on one condition." He leaned back and crossed his arms over his chest.

"What's that?"

"You have to take half and agree to become my new business partner."

"Business partner?" she asked incredulously.

"Yeah, I know you love being in the military, but they don't appreciate you. Luther and I came up with a plan, a business plan, and all we need is someone with your experience and knowledge to help us pull it off."

"I don't love it."

"We still have some things to work out, but it's a solid plan."

"No, I don't love the military anymore. I resigned my position today, just now. In fact, it looks like I could use a job."

"You did? Why?"

"I realized there were other things more important to me. Like self-esteem. You were right, I am just another number, and I deserve more. I deserve to be happy, and I deserve a chance at l-love." There, she'd said it.

"You bet your sweet ass you do. You deserve a hell of a lot more than you've been given. You deserve me."

"And do I have you? And I don't mean as a business partner."

"Body, heart, and soul. You always have. I love you Lara. I want you forever."

"Oh, Riley, I love you too." Lara hooked her foot around his ankle and dropped him to the floor where she straddled him. "And I think it's about time I showed you how much."

"Now that is a plan I can get behind."

"Maybe later."

Lara's body ached for his. Somehow, some way, without her even knowing it, Riley had crept into her soul and claimed it for his own. There was no turning back. Not that she wanted to anyway.

No. Her body knew the one and only man who could satisfy it was under her right now, and whether he was a pirate or a squad leader, he was all she ever wanted.

But that didn't mean he could get complacent about it.

"Remember how you talked about a bondage fantasy?" Lara unfastened his shirt and pushed it back, licking her way down his chest. She very carefully left his arms in the sleeves.

"Uh, yeah." Riley's cock jumped in his pants.

"Well, I have one of my own."

Before he had a chance to figure out what she was up to, Lara wrapped the ends of his shirt around a nearby pipe and tied them tight.

"Hey! Wait a minute! I didn't mean *I* wanted to be tied up."

"You can have your turn later, if you're a very good boy."

Lara stood up and began peeling her formal uniform off slowly. Staring at Riley's muscled chest as she removed her clothes was getting her more than just a little aroused. It had been so long since she felt him. She wanted to touch him everywhere.

"I'm always good. Is this your way of getting even for that spanking I gave you at the *One-eyed-snake*?"

"No, I kind of enjoyed that actually. This is just because I missed you so sparking much that I want to touch you everywhere and as soon as you touch me it's all over."

"So this isn't just to torture me?" Riley's eyes gleamed emerald fire.

"That's just a side benefit." Lara smirked as she pulled off the last of her uniform and went to work on his pants.

Once he was completely naked, she leaned back and just admired her handiwork for a minute. Riley was exposed to her, with his rock-hard cock pulsing and ready for her, jutting up from between his legs. His arms were stretched over his head, showcasing his muscled abs and sexy torso. Just looking at him was stimulating enough to make her wet.

She planned to do a lot more than look.

"Do you know how much I've missed you? I got kinda used to waking up next to you."

"Good. I plan on keeping it that way for the rest of your life. But I'd like to do a little more than sleep next to you now. Come here." His voice was husky with need, and his pupils were dilated with desire.

A shiver of awareness shimmied down her back.

"Oh, I will. Eventually."

Starting at his foot, Lara nibbled and kissed her way up his leg until she reached his inner thigh. The temptation to nuzzle his balls while she was there was almost overwhelming, but she resisted and moved back to the other foot.

"You're killing me, woman!"

"That's the point."

She let her hands drift up ahead of her mouth until they rested on his hips. There, she twirled patterns with her fingers while her mouth moved all around his cock and balls, but never touched them. Breathing moist air over his sac, she gave it one quick lick, then moved to his chest, straddling his hips so her ass grazed his cock.

"I think you're enjoying this far too much." Riley leaned up as much as his arms would allow to draw a nipple into his mouth.

"Aren't you?" Lara's breath caught as he bit her nipple.

"I'd enjoy it more if I could touch you, taste you."

"You're doing a pretty good job of that now." She leaned forward so he could take more of her into his mouth.

"I want to taste your sweet juices. I want to lick your clit while my fingers pump inside your pussy and you come so hard I can feel it. I want to drown in the cream that runs from your body as you climax."

If he kept talking like that, she'd be coming on the spot. "And you will, soon."

Lara pulled away from his tempting lips and licked her way down to his belly button. His cock was practically blue from need, and pre-come pearled at the tip. She had to taste him.

Climbing on top of him, Lara slid down until her pussy was pressed against his face. With a quick moment of thanks for her height, she reached forward and pulled Riley's cock into her mouth while stroking his balls with her other hand. She could feel his breath against her soaking wet clit and groaned as she slid faster over his length.

It wasn't long before Lara felt Riley's tongue stabbing into her center, and the already out of control lust spiraled even higher. Sucking him deeper into her mouth, Lara pumped up and down Riley's cock in time with the furious beating of her heart. Just when she thought she'd explode from the sheer ecstasy of touching and being touched by Riley again, Lara felt something much harder than his tongue pierce her pussy.

"What the—?" Lara lifted her head from Riley's crotch and looked over her shoulder.

Riley's arms were free and his finger was dipping in and out of her pussy.

"You know these synthetic fabrics are slippery. They don't hold a knot for anything." His emerald-green eyes gleamed at her from between her legs as he continued to apply himself to her pussy.

"Darn."

Lara grabbed his cock and stroked it as waves and waves of fire zeroed in between her legs. Riley slid another finger into her pussy and licked harder, bringing her to the edge before he pulled her back again.

Stroking his balls, Lara nipped lightly up and down his cock, silently encouraging him to send her flying. Instead, Riley lightly ran his fingers over the crevice of her ass. Heat slammed into her center and she was almost afraid she'd drown Riley with the juices streaming from her pussy at this new attack on her senses.

Pressure, heat and mind-numbing pleasure swamped Lara's senses. Her body was on a crash course with a supernova and there was nothing she could do, *would* do to stop it.

"Riley!"

"Go with it, baby. I'll catch you when you come down."

Lara pressed her face into the shallow of Riley's hip as the waves of sensation took her soaring. A tapping of fingers around her anus added fuel to the already raging inferno engulfing her. Another finger stroked deep inside her as Riley sucked voraciously on her clit. As he pressed harder, Lara's body exploded in never-ending starbursts of pleasure that reverberated over and over again.

"Holy sparking hell! I think I've died." Lara didn't know if she'd ever move again. Or if she even wanted to.

"*Feck*, I hope not 'cause my balls are so full I'm about to come a geyser."

Riley rolled her over and climbed on top of her, sliding his pulsing cock into her dripping pussy.

"I can get behind that plan," Lara said, locking her arms around his neck and thrusting her hips in time with his strokes.

"Maybe later."

Epilogue

"Thank you for using R.L.L. Superior Services, I hope your journey was safe and enjoyable," Riley said into the microphone of the ship. Lara escorted the dignitary out of the *Bonny Girl 2* and into the hands of his personal security team. Providing personal security to minor royalty had turned out to be a lucrative job. More profitable than smuggling even, not to mention that it still held the occasional surprise or two to keep the adrenaline pumping and the heart rate up. Life was pretty good these days.

Lara walked into the cabin and shook her hair out of its braid. As she bent over, Riley got a fantastic view of her sweet ass in the pseudo-leather pants she wore while on duty. Life was good indeed.

"Well, Prince Harmin is safe and sound, and probably has a few suggestions for his own security personnel. Another satisfied customer."

"I know someone else who could use a little satisfaction." Riley grinned, pointing to his hard-on.

"You know our motto here at R.L.L Superior Services, we aim to please." She strutted across the room to where he was sitting in the captain's chair, unbuttoning her shirt as she went. When she was still feet away from him, she dropped it to the floor and went to work on the pants, kicking her boots off at the same time. She turned around and bent over at the waist while pushing the tight pants off. Her gorgeous butt was inches from his face, and he could do nothing more than stare.

As she peeled her underwear down her long, silky legs, she looked at him over her shoulder, obviously enjoying the torment she was causing. "What's taking you so long? You still have your pants on."

Riley jumped up and pushed his pants down around his ankles, not even bothering with his boots. Before he could get fully situated, Lara pushed him back in the chair and climbed on top of him. Her hot, wet walls gripped him as he began to slide into her waiting pussy.

"I think you like being on top; you seem to push me around an awful lot."

"Once an officer, always an officer. And a good commander always takes care of the man under her. Now move your ass!" She began pumping harder, squeezing his cock with her inner muscles.

"I never thought following orders could be so much fun." Riley dug his hands into her hips, thrusting his dick harder and deeper inside her. When she made the little whimpering sound in the back of her throat that usually preceded her orgasm, he picked her up and laid her on the floor.

"Then again, I always was one for insubordination." He pressed his hand to a spot above her pelvic bone, pushing with his cock from the other side, trying to hit all her hot spots. When her hips flew off the floor and she called his name in a shuddering cry, he knew he had. Letting his own orgasm flow, he felt her muscles milking him, and knew he'd finally struck it rich in all the ways that mattered.

"I love you so much, Riley. More than I ever thought possible." Lara stroked his hair back from his face.

Yup, he was a rich man indeed.

* * * * *

"Hey, Lara! Get over here; you've got to see this!" Riley called from the communication room.

"Again? I think I've seen just about everything you have to show me." Lara smiled to herself as she finished brushing out her hair and headed to the front of the ship. If there was anything guaranteed to get Riley moving it was a direct challenge to his sexual prowess. Not that he needed any.

"We'll discuss that later. Come here and check out this transmission I intercepted."

"Transmission? What type of transmission?"

"See for yourself, I saved it."

What was he up to? Lara pressed play and waited for the screen to come back up. The transmission was foggy and full of static, like it was being sent through a magnetic field or something.

"I can't see a sparking thing on this."

"Just wait, it's coming, hold on." His eyes held a sparkle she was beginning to associate with pending adventure — or disaster.

"—repeat, this is Captain Drog of *The Federation* sending out a distress call from an uncharted planet in the Beta Quad—" there was more static and Lara's gut clenched as she waited to see if it would clear up.

"—have established relations with the indigenous population. Requesting transport from any Imperial ship in the area—"

"Drog! That's my second-in-command! If he's still alive, that means some others must have survived too! Come on, we've got to go find them!"

"I'm way ahead of you, babe. I already put in the request for fuel and logged our route." His hands were busy on the controls, setting their course for the Beta Quadrant.

"That's what I love about you, Flyboy, you don't waste any time." Lara threw back her hair and ran a preliminary check of their supplies.

"Now don't get your hopes up, this call could have gone out months ago. We don't know what we'll find, or even if we can find them. Most of Beta Quad is still unexplored and *fecking* hazardous."

He might be telling her not to get her hopes up, but his eyes weren't any less shiny.

"If Drog's alive, then others are alive too. And if they're out there, I'm going to find them."

"We're going to find them." Riley shot her a smile and initiated takeoff procedures.

And she thought their adventures had come to an end, looked like they were starting off on yet another one. Together.

The End

Enjoy this excerpt from
SILVER FIRE
© Copyright Arianna Hart, 2005

All Rights Reserved, Ellora's Cave, Inc.

Psychic Faylene Driscol has worked for the police department for a long time, but never in all those years has she seen the level of depravity she witnessed after interrogating a Keeper of the Race. This insane cult is out to destroy any non-human — and anyone who'd defend them.

Werewolf Thaddeus Ma'wrl knows all about the Keepers. They killed his entire pack, leaving him a lone wolf out for revenge. Although he'd sworn never to trust another human woman again, he must protect Faylene so she can help put the Keepers behind bars. What he didn't expect was that she'd touch a part of him he'd thought long dead and buried.

As Thad and Faylene run from danger, an irresistible attraction curls between them. Faylene longs to heal the emotional scars Thad carries with him, but she can't help him if he doesn't want her to, and she has her own scars she's hiding. With the Keepers gunning for them, falling in love is the last thing that should be on their minds. Too bad passion makes its own rules and doesn't care about good timing.

Chapter One
New York City, 2112

Even after all these years of looking into the filth that the human brain could hold, it still surprised Faylene Driscoll that one person could live with such raw sewage between his ears. She'd known what she was in for when she'd hired on with the NYPD paranormal division, but nothing had prepared her for the reality of being a human lie detector.

Staying within sight of the security cameras outside the precinct house, Faylene walked in circles in the pool of illumination cast by the floating globe of light above her. She took deep breaths of night air and tried to engage the cleansing rituals that were taught to all psychics almost from birth. No matter how hard she tried to flush out the vile thoughts she'd picked up from the deranged murderer they'd interrogated, the madness remained.

"Damn it! Get out of my head!" Faylene kicked at a pebble on the walk. Okay, try it again. Find her center. Inhale clean, refreshing thoughts, and hold it. Exhale disgusting, foreign thoughts. Again. Stay grounded. Focus only on the act of breathing.

Ten times. After ten times the thoughts should be gone, but she was afraid the images she'd picked up would remain burned on her brain for eternity. How could any human, any *being*, feel that way about another living thing?

And if what she'd "heard" was right, there were hundreds more than they'd ever suspected out there on the streets.

Baby killers.

Only they didn't see it that way. The Keepers of the Race thought they were doing humanity a favor by destroying any man, woman, or child who wasn't one hundred percent human. And anyone who dared to support the species equality laws was fair game as well.

Her stomach rolled again at the hatred and violence contained in one man's head. He'd looked like any other person walking down the street. Tall, skinny, even somewhat attractive, but inside his head seethed madness.

God! Would she ever be able to shake the images?

"Faylene? You coming back in or heading home?" Captain Rogers, her supervisor, called from the steps of the precinct house.

"I'm coming in, just taking a breather." Like any amount of air would scrub her mind clean.

"Don't stay out too long." The Captain nodded his head at her and turned around.

Faylene waited until he was out of sight before she rubbed her hands over her face and tried to find her center again. Maybe this time it would work.

The first breath had barely had a chance to settle in her lungs when a hand covered her mouth and an arm wrapped around her throat. Panic clawed its way to her chest and she couldn't breathe. The arm pressed against her windpipe cutting off her air!

She was dragged roughly into the alley next to the precinct, her throat screamed in agony from the pressure on it. Faylene clutched at the arm that strangled her and fought for air, but her attacker was too strong.

"Stay still, bitch, or I'll snap your neck like a twig." The voice hissed in her ear and sent chills of fear down her back.

Think! She wasn't strong enough to fight him hand-to-hand, but she could use what weapons she had available to her. Concentrating her energies on his shields, Faylene probed his mind looking for a way to attack.

Hate! Anger! Pain! Wave after wave of madness rolled over her, dragging her down in the undertow of its insanity. Oh God! The mental attack hit harder than the physical one. She was going under for the third time.

"Now we're going to step out in front of the cameras and you're going to tell those other dog-lovers to release my private to me or I'll kill you right in front of them."

It was another Keeper! No wonder his mind felt the same. Faylene's head throbbed with pain from the battering of hatred pounding on it. His breath spewed hot and moist air against her cheek as he pulled her in front of the roaming cameras that surrounded the building.

Visions of herself naked and spread facedown on the sidewalk came at her from his mind. Faylene slammed her shields down on the rape fantasy coming from the Keeper and fought the panic that threatened to overwhelm her.

Think! There had to be a way out of this. She'd snap her own neck before she let this bastard fulfill that fantasy.

Just when Faylene was about to gnaw on the bitter-tasting hand holding her captive, the heel of her shoe got caught on a crack in the *plasti-seal* walk and she stumbled forward.

"Clumsy bitch—" His oath was cut off by a rumbling snarl. A hard body barreled into them and threw Faylene sideways.

Not wasting time trying to figure out what happened, Faylene scrambled up on trembling legs and ran for the shelter of the precinct. Tears of fear and relief streamed down her face as she raced up the steps and pounded on the front door. Almost sobbing in frustration, she punched the emergency alarm and pulled frantically at the door.

"Help!" Her heart pounded in her chest and the blood raced in her head. She hit the door again, harder. Didn't anybody look at those damn security monitors? What was the point of having a million freaking cameras around if no one even looked at them?

Alarm sirens screeched around her and lights flashed brightly over the grounds. Faylene almost hit the ground again when a troop of cops in riot gear stormed out of the building. Guns flashed as officers scrambled to find the threat.

No one was there.

"Faylene? What the hell happened?" Captain Rogers pulled her into the tiny entryway.

"Keeper...grabbed me." Her hands were shaking and her breath came in tiny gasps of air. "I tripped, then something hit me and I ran. Didn't look back."

"You'd better sit down. You're bleeding and shaky, probably in shock." Rogers eased her to the floor then ran to the door. "I need a medic in here! Fontain, look for a single male on the premises."

He came back and shuffled his feet in front of her while she took deep breaths and tried to calm her racing pulse.

"Just give me a minute to catch my breath. I'll be fine." Some help she was. Everyone else was out looking for her attacker, and she was sitting on the floor trying not to curl into the fetal position.

"Did you see who attacked you? How do you know it was a Keeper?"

The Captain was tightly shielded so Faylene couldn't tell if he was doing his job or didn't believe her.

"I didn't get a good look at him. He grabbed me from behind and dragged me into the alley. It was dark, I couldn't see him." Her heart sped up again as she remembered the arm across her throat.

"Did he have any distinguishing characteristics? A tattoo, a scar?"

"I told you, I couldn't see him. It all happened so fast. I was trying to clear my head from the interrogation, and the next thing I know, something equally as vile is attacking my brain."

"Attacking your brain?" The Captain raised an eyebrow at her.

"Everyone has a… I don't know… A flavor to their thoughts when they aren't shielding them. This guy had the same nasty flavor as the Keeper inside." It was the coppery taste of blood and death. Faylene shuddered.

"But does that mean he's a Keeper? I can't go after this guy on something as vague as 'he tasted the same way'."

Tinges of bitter sarcasm tainted the Captain's normally bland thoughts. Faylene knew Rogers wasn't thrilled to have a paranormal division in his precinct, but he'd always been a professional before. Did he secretly agree with the narrow-minded dinosaurs who wanted to keep the psychics out of the mainstream?

"I know he's a Keeper because he was using me as a hostage to get his private back." Faylene pulled herself up off the floor and looked Rogers in the eye. No wonder he didn't take her seriously. She'd been huddled on the floor like a quivering mass of gelatin.

"He said that?" Rogers typed furiously into his *wrist comm*.

"His exact words escape me, but it was something to the effect of 'tell those other dog-lovers to release my private or I'll snap your neck'."

"Looks like this might be worse than I thought. So what happened? How'd you get away?"

"I tripped over a crack in the walk and someone—or something—slammed into us. I ran away and hit the emergency alarm."

"We'll review the visual and see what it was. Why don't you go and get cleaned up? I'll let you know if we find any signs of this guy. Are you going to press charges?"

"Damn straight I am."

Faylene stalked off to the bathroom to clean up the blood that oozed from the cuts on her hands and knees. Her hose were ruined. So much for being indestructible. Science could produce crops on the moon base, but couldn't make a decent pair of pantyhose.

Peeling the torn, bloody garments down her legs, Faylene inspected the damage. Not too bad. She'd have some spectacular bruises in a few days, and the scrapes would look nasty for a while, but nothing broken or sprained.

She still had the taste of the Keeper's hand in her mouth, and in her brain.

At least she could rinse the taste out of her mouth.

Faylene rifled through the little basket of toiletries under the sink for some mouthwash, or mints, or toothpaste, anything to rid her of the flavor of the Keeper's hand. A half-empty pack of gum lay under some bobby pins and an unused nail file. She pounced on it and stuffed three pieces in her mouth at once.

Walking out of the bathroom, Faylene almost got trampled by the cops coming back into the building. A few strange looks were cast her way, but no one said anything to her.

"Did you find anything?" Faylene asked Rogers as he broke away from the conversation he was having with another cop.

"Not a damn thing. We're going to check the recordings now."

The look he gave her practically screamed disbelief. Screw him. She hadn't gotten these scrapes from her imagination. Someone *did* grab her. And someone else *did* save her.

Faylene followed Rogers to the surveillance room. Shielding for all she was worth, she clamped down on her thoughts and let none of her nervousness show. She would not look like a hysterical female in front of a room full of alpha males. It was bad enough they already thought she was imagining things. She didn't need to make them think she was a girlie-girl too.

Two cops who were close to retirement age manned the surveillance room. Dozens of monitors flashed different camera angles of the area around the precinct house.

Ever since the riots of 2100, security around police stations had increased significantly. Police officers had become prime targets for every antiestablishment cause that had more than three supporters. With the new security in place, no movement within a hundred meters should go unrecorded.

Should being the operative word. Someone had gotten past the monitors and alarms and had gotten close enough to grab her. Two someones, actually.

"Hey, Joe, can you bring up the video from half an hour ago on the 'A' side of the building?"

Faylene watched the recording of herself walking around in circles on the black and white monitor. No wonder everyone was shooting her strange looks, she looked like a spooked horse!

If they had "seen" what she had seen inside that Keeper's head, they'd be spooked too.

Her stomach rolled at the memory and she had to fight down the bile that rose in her throat. Rogers appeared on the screen briefly before it fuzzed and skipped. When the image came back, Faylene saw herself disheveled and running to the alarm.

"What the hell happened?" Rogers leaned over to the control panel and tapped some keys. "Where's the time log on this thing?"

"Nothing showed up?"

"Look, here's the time stamp. The section from 0012 to 0016 is missing. Check the other cameras."

The surveillance crew pulled up recording after recording, and the same four minutes were missing on every one.

"Son of a bitch! Someone must have a scrambler or something! How could this happen? This is supposed to be top of the line technology."

"Wait! What's that?" Faylene grabbed Joe's shoulder. "Pull that angle back to 0018, I think I saw something." She waited anxiously to see if there really was something there.

"There it is! See that flash. Can you slow it down?"

"Lady, I can slow it down, speed it up, and even make it dance for you."

Joe manipulated the recording until it went frame by frame, and even then Faylene almost missed seeing the figure.

"Stop! Enlarge that frame right there."

With a few taps of the keys, the image on screen got bigger and bigger. Gradually a man appeared. Faylene's breath caught in her throat as the picture grew clearer. He was big and muscular, stocky with wide shoulders.

But it wasn't his physique that caught her attention. Or even the scar that ran down his forehead over the corner of one eye and across his cheekbone. It was the feral snarl that made his lip curl and revealed the fangs underneath that held her spellbound. "Fangs!"

"What?" Rogers leaned closer to the screen.

"He has fangs, look there." Faylene had never seen fangs on a human before.

"He's a Were. Probably wolf by the look of him."

"How can you tell?" Faylene tried to move closer, too. The eyes blazing at her from the monitor captured her and wouldn't let go. Something in that face screamed of such pain and bone-deep sadness she couldn't look away.

"See the shape of his face? High cheekbones, broad forehead, and a wide jaw. If he were a Vamp or a Cat he'd have a narrower face. Plus he's stocky like a wolf. Vamps and cats are more wiry."

"I didn't realize there were so many differences." Faylene hadn't had many dealings with the city's Were population, they pretty much kept to themselves in their enclaves. The packs policed themselves and avoided contact with authorities.

"Fucking dogs," Joe mumbled just loud enough for them to hear.

"What was that?" Rogers barked.

"Nothing, sir." Joe stared straight ahead and didn't say another word, but Faylene could feel the hatred and fear coming from him.

She'd felt the same emotions whenever the discussion turned to the para-population. Differences scared people. Politicians could talk all they wanted about New York being a melting pot for all species, it didn't change the fear and mistrust in people's hearts.

"We'll put out an APB on this guy and have our teams bring him in."

"No!" Faylene said sharply. "I mean, he isn't the one who grabbed me. He saved me from the Keeper."

"How can you tell?" Rogers looked at her dubiously.

"The man who grabbed me wanted to kill Weres, he was human and wanted to get rid of anything that wasn't human."

"Still, I'll want to ask him a few questions. He managed to get on the grounds without being detected by the cameras, and I want to know how."

Rogers stood and stretched his back. "You might as well go home and get some sleep. I'll need you here first thing in the morning when we question the Keeper again."

Faylene shuddered at the thought of going back into the cesspool of the Keeper's mind.

"That is, if you think you can handle it."

Faylene lifted her chin and looked him straight in the eye. "I can handle it. I'll be back here at 0900, Captain." Whether she liked it or not.

* * * * *

A scratching on her bedroom window pulled Faylene out of a nightmare. In her dream she was running and running, but she couldn't see what was chasing her. It took her a minute to realize the tapping on her window was real.

There was no way she was going to wait and find out if it was friend or foe. Faylene grabbed her *wrist comm* off the nightstand and raced from the room. Before she got to the hallway, her window burst open in a shower of glass.

"Don't run! They're waiting for you outside."

The voice was deep and raspy, almost a snarl. Faylene faltered in her tracks. Her heart pounded and she went weak in the knees. Without looking she knew who it was. The werewolf from the precinct house stood in her bedroom.

Slowly turning around, Faylene looked at her intruder. She had her finger poised on the emergency button of her *wrist comm*, but something held her back.

He'd saved her before, maybe he was trying to help her again?

The face she recognized from the vid at the precinct, but black and white had hidden a hell of a lot. The security camera couldn't capture the pure vitality radiating from him, nor the pulsing heat of his aura.

"Who's waiting for me, and who are you?" she asked. Her knees shook, and she hoped he wouldn't notice.

"The Keepers are waiting for you."

Faylene noticed his eyes gleamed silver, as did the streak of hair that shone in his otherwise black mop.

"Why should I believe you? You broke into my apartment! You could be trying to kill me yourself for all I know." Even as she said the words, she knew they weren't true. His aura radiated pain and sadness, and even some restrained violence, but he wasn't a killer. That much she'd stake her life on.

"If I had wanted to kill you, Faylene, you'd be dead by now. I could have taken out your throat before you ever made it to the door."

Fear shot through her and Faylene edged closer to the door. "How do you know my name? And what are you doing here?"

"I've read about you in the paper. You're the prosecutor's only chance for putting the Keepers away."

"That doesn't explain what you're doing here, in my bedroom."

He looked so out of place amidst her ice blue silk and floral patterns. Her room was her sanctuary. She filled it with feminine, calming influences. He was anything but calm or feminine. Red-hot male filled her private space and took it over.

"I've been following you. Making sure the Keepers wouldn't hurt you."

"You've been following me!" Hot anger took the place of fear as indignation washed over her.

"Yes. The Keepers have to be stopped, and you're the only one who can put them away. I'll do anything to make sure you stay alive. Including standing here arguing with you when we should be running."

Before Faylene could ask any more questions, the window to her tiny living room broke with a crash. There was a whoosh of air, and heat scorched her as flames engulfed the room.

"To the roof! Come on!"

In a blur of movement too fast for her to follow, he grabbed her and threw her over his shoulder. He was solid as a rock, and Faylene could feel the muscles of his shoulder and back bunch and roll as he moved. She could hear the tinkling of shattering glass as he cleared the broken window of the dangerous shards. Before Faylene could protest, they were out of the bedroom window and he began climbing up the building with her slung over his shoulder.

"At least tell me your name." Faylene tried to right her spinning world as the ground disappeared rapidly beneath her.

The musky smell of him hit her hard. A shot of lust went through her like a lightning bolt. It occurred to her that she was only in a pair of oversized men's boxer shorts and a thin tank top with not a stitch of underwear on. She was instantly conscious of the thin cotton of her shorts being the only thing separating her pussy from his shoulder.

"Just call me Thad. We'll have formal introductions later," he grunted as he climbed onto the roof of her apartment building and set her on her feet.

"There they are! On the roof!" A shout came from the ground below, and bullets whizzed by Faylene's head.

"Run!" Thad grabbed her arm and pulled her across the rooftop, hauling her along when she stumbled.

Faylene tried to keep up with Thad as he dodged objects she could barely see in the dark. They were rapidly running out of room when another blaze of fire flared up right behind them.

"Get ready to jump!" he shouted as they came to the edge of her building.

"Jump? Are you out of your mind? It's at least three meters between buildings, I can't jump that far!"

The words had barely left her mouth before she went flying through the air. She didn't dare look down to see if they were going to make it to the neighboring building, but squeezed her eyes closed. The impact of their landing jolted the breath out of her lungs, but Thad didn't give her time to recover before he pulled her up again.

"Come on, we'll take the fire escape to the street and get away through the tunnels."

Faylene didn't even bother asking what tunnels. She needed all her air to keep up with him and escape the lunatics who were throwing firebombs at her.

The darkness of the night hid the ground below them and Faylene felt a shiver of fear go through her as they climbed down. It was probably a good thing she couldn't see how far up they were. She wasn't real fond of heights, but she was less fond of bullets and being burnt alive.

"This way." Thad grabbed her hand, his much larger one swallowing hers up. A flash of heat shot through her followed by a brief glimpse of pain. Faylene gasped at the conflicting sensations swirling through her head before he cut off the connection. Something had hurt this man at a bone-deep level. Hurt him so badly that even when he was shielded and running for his life, pain was still with him.

Thad led her to a manhole cover that he lifted with an inhuman display of strength. Faylene watched in awe as his muscles jumped and bulged as he hefted the heavy cover.

"Down there, quickly."

Faylene scrambled down a rusty ladder bolted to the side of the tunnel. She didn't even want to think about what she was stepping in with bare feet. When she got to the bottom rung she hesitated. God only knew what was waiting for her on the ground.

There was a grating of metal on metal and the last sliver of light was extinguished. A brush of air swirled by her and Faylene caught the smell of Thad briefly before she felt hands on her hips.

"I'll carry you, this is no place to be walking in bare feet."

"How'd you get down here so fast?" Faylene asked. His hands on her hips sent a jolt of lust straight to her crotch.

"I jumped," he said simply. "Come on, I'll take us someplace safe and get you some suitable clothes."

He jumped? It was at least two meters down and he'd landed without a sound? She definitely needed to learn more about Werewolves and their talents. Faylene had a feeling there was more to it than howling at the moon once a month.

About the author:

Arianna Hart lives on the East Coast with her husband and three daughters. When not teaching, writing, or chasing after her children and the dog, Ari likes to practice her karate, go for long walks, and read by the pool. She thinks heaven is having a good book, warm sun, and a drink in her hand. Until she can sit down long enough to enjoy all three, she'll settle for the occasional hour of peace and quiet.

Arianna Hart welcomes mail from readers. You can write to her c/o Ellora's Cave Publishing at 1337 Commerce Drive, Suite 13, Stow OH 44224.

Why an electronic book?

We live in the Information Age—an exciting time in the history of human civilization in which technology rules supreme and continues to progress in leaps and bounds every minute of every hour of every day. For a multitude of reasons, more and more avid literary fans are opting to purchase e-books instead of paperbacks. The question to those not yet initiated to the world of electronic reading is simply: *why?*

1. *Price.* An electronic title at Ellora's Cave Publishing runs anywhere from 40-75% less than the cover price of the <u>exact same title</u> in paperback format. Why? Cold mathematics. It is less expensive to publish an e-book than it is to publish a paperback, so the savings are passed along to the consumer.

2. *Space.* Running out of room to house your paperback books? That is one worry you will never have with electronic novels. For a low one-time cost, you can purchase a handheld computer designed specifically for e-reading purposes. Many e-readers are larger than the average handheld, giving you plenty of screen room. Better yet, hundreds of titles can be stored within your new library—a single microchip. (Please note that Ellora's Cave does not endorse any specific brands. You can check our website at www.ellorascave.com for customer recommendations we make available to new consumers.)

3. *Mobility*. Because your new library now consists of only a microchip, your entire cache of books can be taken with you wherever you go.

4. *Personal preferences are accounted for*. Are the words you are currently reading too small? Too large? Too...**ANNOYING**? Paperback books cannot be modified according to personal preferences, but e-books can.

5. *Innovation*. The way you read a book is not the only advancement the Information Age has gifted the literary community with. There is also the factor of what you can read. Ellora's Cave Publishing will be introducing a new line of interactive titles that are available in e-book format only.

6. *Instant gratification.* Is it the middle of the night and all the bookstores are closed? Are you tired of waiting days — sometimes weeks — for online and offline bookstores to ship the novels you bought? Ellora's Cave Publishing sells instantaneous downloads 24 hours a day, 7 days a week, 365 days a year. Our e-book delivery system is 100% automated, meaning your order is filled as soon as you pay for it.

Those are a few of the top reasons why electronic novels are displacing paperbacks for many an avid reader. As always, Ellora's Cave Publishing welcomes your questions and comments. We invite you to email us at service@ellorascave.com or write to us directly at: 1337 Commerce Drive, Suite 13, Stow OH 44224.

Discover for yourself why readers can't get enough of the multiple award-winning publisher Ellora's Cave. Whether you prefer e-books or paperbacks, be sure to visit EC on the web at www.ellorascave.com for an erotic reading experience that will leave you breathless.

WWW.ELLORASCAVE.COM

Printed in the United States
28151LVS00002B/238-249